FRENEMIES

FRENEMIES

ALEXA YOUNG

RANDOM HOUSE AUSTRALIA

A Random House book
Published by Random House Australia Pty Ltd
Level 3, 100 Pacific Highway, North Sydney NSW 2060
www.randomhouse.com.au

First published in the USA by HarperTeen, an imprint of HarperCollins
Publishers
First published by Random House Australia in 2009

alloyentertainment
Produced by Alloy Entertainment
151 West 26th St, New York, NY 10001

Addresses for companies within the Random House Group can be found at
www.randomhouse.com.au/offices.

National Library of Australia
Cataloguing-in-Publication Entry

Author: Young, Alexa
Title: Frenemies / Alexa Young
ISBN: 978 1 74166 412 6 (pbk.)
Series: Frenemies; 1
Target Audience: For secondary school age
Dewey Number: 813

Cover design by Ellie Exarchos
Cover photography by Getty Images
Internal design by Andrea C. Uva
Printed and bound by The SOS Print + Media Group

10 9 8 7 6 5 4 3 2

For Joel and Jack

Missed you, love you, mean it

*H*alley Brandon had survived the impossible: two whole months away from her best friend in the world. But now she was finally home.

Her mom had barely stopped her champagne-colored Mercedes CLK convertible before Halley was out the car door, racing through her family's ultramodern living room toward the backyard that bordered Avalon Greene's property.

She slipped through the sun-bleached wood gate and tip-toed along the edge of the Greenes' sparkling infinity pool, the water shining like a smooth aquamarine gemstone in the warm Southern California sun. Avalon was reading in her usual spot beside the mosaic-tiled patio table—her long, straight blond hair shielding her face like a veil. Up until this summer, Halley had spent every June, July, and August right here, sipping Snapple Peach Iced Tea and challenging

Avalon to swim-offs. But last spring she'd applied to UC Berkeley's Inkubator Art Program and couldn't *not* go once she'd been lucky enough to get accepted to California's most exclusive art camp. At first, Avalon didn't get what an honor it was for Halley to get in and tried to convince her not to go, but eventually she understood and was totally happy for her friend.

Halley silently sank into her favorite chaise lounge and let out a sigh. "Nice day, isn't it?"

"Ohmygod!" Avalon leapt up from her chair. "You're *here!*" She ran over and dove onto Halley, smothering her best friend with a monster hug. Both girls giggled as Halley tried to blink back the tears that were beginning to well up in her intense blue eyes.

"So!" Avalon stood, reaching her arms out to Halley. "I can't believe you're really back!"

"I really am!" Halley laughed and quickly ran a finger under her bottom lashes before letting Avalon pull her off the chaise.

"I missed you like crazy." Avalon shook her head dramatically and cast her deep Hershey Kiss–colored eyes down at her perfectly French-pedicured toenails. "It was *awful* without you."

"I know, but—" Just as Halley was about to tell Avalon every detail about every minute she'd spent in Berkeley, she heard a bark and turned to see the girls' golden retriever–mix puppy, Pucci—named for the favorite designer of Constance Greene and Abigail Brandon, a.k.a. "The Moms"—rounding the back of the Greenes' saffron-hued Spanish-style house. In a replay of Avalon's tackle from a minute ago, Pucci leapt onto Halley and covered her with sloppy wet kisses.

"Oh, Pucci! I missed you, too, my little Pucci-poochy-pooch!" Halley wrapped her arms around the puppy and sank back onto the lounge chair. "I can't believe how big you've gotten!"

Pucci woofed at Avalon, and Halley looked up at her best friend again.

"Ohmygod—Pucci's not the *only* one who's bigger!" Halley practically screamed, staring at her best friend's chest. Avalon's A-cups had practically doubled in size since July.

Avalon grimaced. "Hey, leave 'the girls' alone."

"I think it's more like 'the *women*' at this point!" Halley stifled a laugh.

"Uh-huh." Avalon's face clouded over slightly.

Halley sensed she'd accidentally stepped onto an Ava-landmine and figured she should start backing out. Quietly. "Well, with or without the new *developments*, you look totally fab!" Halley grinned, relaxing back into the chaise. "You're *so* tan, and that skirt is *awesome*. Where'd you find it?"

"Thanks. It's Stella McCartney. I know we're not discount shoppers, but I heard about this crazy influx of Stella pieces at Nordstrom Rack in July. I couldn't resist!" Avalon tilted

3

her head. Her eyes traveled from Halley's long, wavy dark locks down to the tips of her vintage lavender leather boots. "Are those . . . *cowboy boots*?"

"Yup!" Halley waited for Avalon to ask her more about her ensemble: a silky gray camisole and black Bermuda shorts with a wide wine-colored belt. The shorts actually belonged to Chad Rollins; stealing them out of the graphic design instructor's room had been her ultimate art camp Truth or Dare moment.

"Wow . . . cute." Avalon wrinkled her nose.

"What?" Halley asked. "Don't you think I'm a complete Yes?"

"Um, sure." Avalon nodded her head and widened her golden-brown eyes innocently.

"Why do I not believe you?"

"Well . . ." Avalon turned to look out at the pool and then spun back to face Halley. "Okay, truth?"

"Of course." Halley and Avalon always told each other the truth—that's what best friends are for, right?

"It's a Maybe at best," Avalon said. "I mean, it *is* like eighty degrees outside—not exactly boot weather—and, hello? You need a little more than purple footwear and accessories to pull off all that gray and black."

Halley couldn't believe her best friend had just Maybe'd her. They'd been playing *Yes, No, Maybe* with virtually every outfit they'd ever seen since the third grade, and Maybes

4

happened only in extreme fashion emergencies—which this was *not*.

"Whatever." Halley shrugged off the style citation. If she knew one thing about her best friend, it was that Avalon didn't like anybody to start a trend before she did. She was probably just jealous. Besides, Avalon was skating dangerously close to a Maybe herself, the way her new boobs were tempting fate under her white halter top.

"*Anyway* . . ." Halley placed her hands behind her head and stretched out on the chaise, eager to move on, while Pucci curled up at her feet and gave her cocoa butter–moisturized calf a lick. "Tell me *everything* I missed while I was gone."

"Ohmygod, *so much!*" Avalon squealed, clapped her hands twice, and began pacing along the edge of the pool in debriefing mode. "We've already got about twelve bat mitzvah invites, and Becca Krasnoff is apparently having Gwen Stefani design her dress. Can you even believe?"

"Seriously?" Halley gasped. "Ohmygod, that's so crazy because—"

"Seriously!" Avalon cut Halley off before she could finish explaining that L.A.M.B. was one of her new favorite labels. "I guess Becca's dad used to work with Gwen's older brother or something. How cool is that?"

Halley grinned and resigned herself to the fact that her art camp stories would have to wait. Avalon was clearly on a roll. She pulled off her boots so she could burrow her bare feet into Pucci's soft blond fur.

"But even cooler?" Avalon continued, barely pausing for breath. "Courtney had her sweet sixteen last week, and since she's style-dyslexic, I totally designed the whole thing."

"It's unbelievable that your sister can actually drive now! Was the party beyond amazing?" Halley separated her dark waves evenly and then twisted each side into a pigtail before tying them together in a knot at the nape of her neck.

"Beyond," Avalon confirmed, pursing her glossy lips in an exaggerated pout. "But I was *so* sad you weren't there. Everyone was."

Halley felt a pang of guilt for having left Avalon alone in La Jolla while she had the greatest summer ever in Berkeley. But at least Avalon had found somewhere to channel all her social energy. Avalon *lived* for parties. Or, at least, for *talking* about parties.

After about twenty minutes of nonstop dishing about her big sister's birthday, Avalon took a deep breath and raised a pale blond eyebrow. "So?"

Halley inhaled, preparing to launch into her moment-by-moment art camp recap.

"Best part?" Avalon went on. "I've decided it's time for *us* to throw a major bash."

"Really?" Halley asked, a little confused, since neither of

their birthdays were coming up and the next partyworthy holiday was Halloween.

"Totally." Avalon ran over to a light pink folder off the patio table and raced back to Halley, standing tall, as if she were delivering an oral report. "Okay! The name of our fabulous fête will be Friendapalooza." She handed Halley the folder emblazoned with sparkly purple letters. "The theme will be fashion—*obvs*! We'll invite all the cutest boys in school, and *you* can design the invitations!"

"Hmmm." Halley tried to hide her uncertainty in the face of Avalon's over-the-top excitement.

"Or we can just do Evites." Avalon grinned, sitting down next to Pucci. "I already started playing around with a few ideas online, and—"

"It's not *that* . . . ," Halley said, still pondering the idea.

"Then *what*?" Avalon demanded. "We've been best friends our entire lives, and what could be more worth celebrating? Plus we've just spent our first summer apart and are, like, seriously independent women now. And finally, as everyone knows, thirteen is the new sixteen."

"Hmmm," Halley said again. It made sense. Sort of. It just seemed a little . . . lame?

"*Pleeeease!*" Avalon grabbed Halley's hand to give it an urgent squeeze. "I am *so close* to getting The Moms to say yes . . . but I *need* you to convince them, too. They'll be so happy you're back that they'll do anything you ask."

Pucci barked. She seemed to agree that a party was in order.

Halley let out a loud sigh and shook her head as she grinned at her best friend. If anyone knew how to get her way, Avalon, daughter of two lawyers, certainly did. She was a master manipulator—in all the best ways, of course.

Of course.

All the news that's fit to wear

*A*valon pulled her printed silk scarf off her head, shaking her long tresses down like a classic movie starlet ready for her close-up.

Or the first day of school.

She and Halley waved good-bye to Pucci, who was riding shotgun with Avalon's mom, and strode toward the terra-cotta-roofed main building of Seaview Middle School, commanding the attention of their classmates. Even the palm trees in front of SMS, a former Mediterranean-style boutique hotel that had been converted into a public school long before Halley and Avalon were even born, seemed to be arching to get a better view of the girls' back-to-school ensembles.

"Hey, Avalon!" someone shouted from the middle of a group of girls standing near the entrance to the Spanish-tiled school lobby.

"Hey, Bree!" Avalon yelled back, pulling Halley over toward Brianna Cho, SMS's head cheerleader. When Halley had left for camp, Avalon worried that she'd be riding her bike to the beach and laying out by the pool alone all summer. Luckily, except for a week at cheer camp, Brianna had stayed in town, too. Even more luckily, Brianna turned out to be a lot of fun.

"You guys look fantastic!" Brianna gushed, tucking a lock of long, satiny black hair behind one ear.

"Thanks." Avalon grinned. "And how cute do *you* look?"

"Really? Yay!" Brianna raised both arms overhead in a V-for-victory pose that revealed a sliver of tan skin between her red babydoll tee and dark-wash denim. She crinkled her button nose and giggled nervously. "So, how was art camp, Halley?"

"Oh, um . . . cool," Halley replied with a puzzled look on her face. "Really great."

"Awesome!" Brianna cheered as the warning bell for first period rang. "Can't wait to hear all about it."

"Uh, sure." Halley didn't even try to hide her bewilderment as Avalon waved to the group of cheerleaders.

"Since when are we friends with Brianna Cho?" Halley whispered as she and Avalon walked through a pair of gold-rimmed sliding-glass doors and into the school lobby, which was awash in old-world charm—from the tiled floors, vaulted ceilings, and crown molding to the wrought-iron chandeliers, hand-carved doors, and dark wood tables boasting vases of fresh orchids.

"Um, since around the time you went away for the whole summer and I had nobody to hang out with." Avalon tried not to sound too annoyed as they slipped out another set of glass doors and strode across the campus green toward journalism class, but it kind of seemed like Halley was questioning her social judgment—and could she have been any ruder to Brianna?

"I wasn't gone for the *whole* summer," Halley said, waving to a tall girl who was rushing toward them along the brick footpath that led out to the campus's sprawling grassy hills and villas reserved for staff offices and the most popular elective classes. The girl squealed an excited "Hey!" in Halley's direction.

Halley's face broke into a grin, and Avalon realized Halley was smiling at *Sofee Hughes*. Avalon got a face full of blond-streaked jet-black curls as the girl raced past them.

Avalon shook her head at the drive-by greeting that had just occurred. "Well, since when do we acknowledge Sofee? She's a severe fashion *No* and completely rude to us."

"We were roommates in Berkeley," Halley said, pushing open the arched mission-style wood door to the journalism villa. "She's actually really cool."

Avalon frowned at Halley as they made their way through the rows of iMacs and past mock-up Web pages of the

SMS.com Daily taped to the chalkboard. Halley had been hanging out with Sofee Hughes at art camp? And she'd decided Sofee—whom they both used to call *Softee* in fifth grade before she grew, like, ten inches and the weight got distributed more evenly—was *cool*? This was going to require a major intervention, not exactly something Avalon could pull off mere minutes before their first class of eighth grade.

"Hey, guys!" Anna Velasquez's auburn bob bounced as the new student body president set down a copy of *People* to give Halley and Avalon quick welcome hugs. Carrie Jackson and Lizbeth Schultz turned from the magazine rack to squeal their hellos, too. Their minidresses accented with leopard-print accessories were clearly inspired by *true* trendsetters—Halley and Avalon. Mark Cohen, last year's top sports reporter, shot the group an approving glance.

"Hey, Anna," Avalon said. "Love your dresses—all of you."

"Thanks." Carrie's wide green eyes and glowing skin made her a miniature replica of a supermodel-era Tyra Banks. "You guys look amazing as always."

"Merci beaucoup!" Halley twirled around in her black tunic and dark denim capris. "We try."

"Oh, please," Lizbeth chimed in shyly. "You guys don't even have to *try*; Halvalon is the definition of style."

Avalon beamed and looked down at her camel-colored loose-fit shorts and preppy argyle vest over puffed-sleeve blouse. She had to admit that she and Halley were both Yes-times-ten today—although things might not have looked so good if she hadn't convinced Halley to swap those weird lavender cowboy boots for a cute pair of red ballet flats, just like the ones Avalon had on.

"Did you see what Margie and Olive are wearing?" Lizbeth whispered with a smirk. She narrowed her teal eyes and tossed a long, fine, strawberry-blond curl behind her pale freckled shoulder.

Halley and Avalon looked toward the front of the room, where the *Daily*'s resident science snobs-slash-health columnists stood, probably plotting a way to top last year's schoolwide germ scare. A faded red-and-black plaid jumper hung from Margie Herring's bony, sloped shoulders. Her coarse dark hair made her nearly translucent skin look blue. Olive Johnson wore a beige-and-yellow version of the same jumper, which matched her frizzy hair. The plaid was pulled tight over her short, pudgy frame.

"My eyes may never recover," Carrie snickered.

"Oh, come on, they look *hot!*" Halley gave Avalon the one-raised-eyebrow signal that she was setting up a fashion bashing.

"Definitely *hot*." Avalon grinned as she watched Carrie's mouth drop open, Lizbeth's eyes widen, and Anna's nose scrunch up in stunned horror. "But you'd be sizzling, too, if you wore decaying wool in the middle of a heat wave!"

The group burst into hysterics as their journalism teacher, Miss Frey, breezed into the room. She was the picture of

13

editorial perfection in oversize Dior sunglasses, a charcoal pencil skirt, and a tailored white button-down oxford. Rumor had it that Miss Frey had gone from a geeky, wiry-haired grade-school reject to a glossy-chignoned college intern for *Elle*. She'd been to New York Fashion Week twice. She had even met Anna. *Anna Wintour*.

After quickly agreeing to meet at the Garden of Serenity for lunch, the girls headed for their seats. Miss Frey took her place at the front of the room and traded her shades for a pair of dark-rimmed Prada glasses.

"Good morning, everyone." Miss Frey smiled warmly and leaned against her desk. "I hope you had a great break and are ready to get back to work—it's time to show this school just how an online daily should be written!"

Several students whistled, and Avalon and Halley exchanged excited glances. Avalon whipped out her super-professional pink-snakeskin embossed folder, full of all the story ideas she'd brainstormed over the summer.

"As usual, I'll expect you all to contribute a variety of articles to the *Daily* this year," Miss Frey continued. "But in addition to your regular reporting duties, we have room for one new feature—a daily column. The topic for it is wide open. The column can be about art, music, fashion, fitness—anything, really—so long as it doesn't overlap with the rest of our content."

"Rock on, Miss Frey!" The *Daily*'s entertainment expert (and Brianna's brother), David Cho, pumped his fist in the air.

14

Avalon's heart felt like it might explode through the diamond pattern on her vest. Miss Frey had looked directly at her and Halley when she said "fashion." When Avalon locked eyes with Halley, she could practically see her best friend's brain working. Even if Halley's smile hadn't threatened to take over her entire face, Avalon would have seen the tiny explosions of excitement in those clear blue eyes.

"You can begin posting your columns tomorrow on the 'Competition' page after seven a.m., so that posts have an equal amount of time to impress readers," Miss Frey said. "You will post every day, and then the school will have the opportunity to vote for their favorite in three weeks. The winner will have a permanent spot in the editorial lineup. So, good luck! I can't wait to see what you all come up with."

The entire villa erupted into a buzz of enthusiastic chatter.

Halley leaned over her desk. "Are we on the same Web page?" she whispered.

"Absolutely," Avalon replied with a grin. Finally, they could launch *Yes, No, Maybe* into cyberspace. After all, people had been taking their fashion cues from Halley and Avalon since third grade. "And I think I know our first victims." She nodded in the direction of Margie and Olive. Avalon watched as the plaid duo put their heads together, planning whatever snoozetastic column they were going to write. "You know, Halley, I really don't think this year can get any better."

Back to Cool

by the Style Snarks

posted: tuesday, 9/9, at 7:18 a.m

Darling Fashionistas: It's a new year, and shouldn't it also be a new you? Then vote for our column, and we'll bring you a daily dose of fashion direction to help you get your wardrobe exactly where it needs to be—and trust us when we say we're not going to pull any punches.

We'll also be telling you what deserves major props (BCBG calfskin messenger bag? YES. Sassy Cynthia Rowley minidress? Double YES. Leopard-print J. Crew flats? YES times *twelve!*) and what screams, "Major *clothes-pas!*" (Wool jumpers in the middle of a heat wave? NO. Satin short-shorts outside of a slumber party? Double NO. Tie-dyed tees, ripped jeans, and Crocs? NO times *infinity.*)

Don't get us wrong. We realize putting together the ultimate fashion statement can be super stressful. And that's why we've put together this debut column designed to school you in the Four C's of Style:

1. **Confidence.** If you hate what you're wearing, then hello? So will everyone else. Always dress according to what you love, and then, say it with us: shoulders back, head high, step, step, step. (P.S. Nobody—except yours truly!—will know your Prada's a fake if you carry it like a gift from Miuccia herself.)

2. **Class.** No, not algebra. If it looks like you've been raiding your toy poodle's wardrobe or we can see your peeping thong (and we don't mean flip-flops) every time you raise your hand, you're going to gain a reputation for being anything but fashion-forward. Leave a little something to the imagination, mmmkay?

3. **Couture.** You don't have to be decked out in head-to-toe designer wear, but accessorizing with a pair of haute shades will transform you from drab to fab in mere seconds. (And FYI: Juicy is cute, but so not couture.)

4. **Confidantes.** Everybody needs a close friend who can tell her what she should and shouldn't wear. Why do you think we always look our best?

That's it! Our secrets are now yours . . . so no more excuses for the rest of the year. In this case, four C's will get you an A in fashion every time.

Oh, and don't forget to vote (for us)! ☺

Word to your closet,   Shop on,
Halley Brandon   *Avalon Greene*

Snarkalicious! ☺ Can't wait to see what u 2 wear 2day.
U will win the column competition 4 sure. Luv ya!

posted by clotheshorse **on 9/9 at 7:25 a.m.**

Juicy is totally couture. Why else do they call it Juicy Couture?
Duh. I'm not voting 4 this column.

posted by hotterthanU **on 9/9 at 7:36 a.m.**

U girls ROCK! So loving this column. U have my vote—and I
know lots of people who will be voting for U too. Go, fight,
win!

posted by cheeriously **on 9/9 at 7:40 a.m.**

OMG . . . so psyched someone who knows how to dress
will be giving the people at this school some fashion pointers.
Can I vote more than once? U R doing a public service.
AWESOME!

posted by madameprez **on 9/9 at 7:43 a.m.**

Snarktastic, girlies! But I might have to vote for Mark's sports
column. It's gonna be a close game!

posted by tuffprincess **on 9/9 at 7:59 a.m.**

Cute boy alert!

"Oh . . . my . . . god. Look . . . at . . . that." Avalon was practically cutting off Halley's circulation as she squeezed her upper arm. "What is Wynter *thinking*?"

Halley had to agree. The girls were standing in the school's landscaped courtyard, warming up for a day of column-campaigning with a few Yes, No, Maybes. Wynter Alexander's long-cream-blouse-over-black-leggings combo would have been sort of Lohan-chic without the monster ruffle on her chest. And Halley couldn't imagine what had possessed her to wear a patterned head scarf. When Halley and Avalon wore vintage scarves, it was a convertible-induced necessity. But Wynter's mother drove a Lexus hybrid SUV.

"It's so tragic." Avalon frowned, sliding her aviator shades down her nose to take a better look. "Somebody has clearly seen *Pirates of the Caribbean* one time too many."

"*And* all the sequels."

"Hey, Wynter—where's the eye patch?" Avalon yelled.

Although Wynter was already safely out of earshot, a cluster of volleyball girls laughed at Avalon's Wynter-vention. "Good one, Avalon," called a bronzed-beyond-belief blocker.

"Thanks, Zoe!" Avalon waved at the burly blond girl in the shiny blue tracksuit.

"But don't get too cocky there, Hulk Hogan," Avalon whispered to Halley. "Your dresser's quite a few drawers short of a *Yes*."

"*Nice!*" Halley nodded her head.

"Ooh . . ." Avalon sucked in her breath and looked over Halley's shoulder. "But *that* is a *definite* Yes!"

"Where?" Halley asked, turning to see Cassidy Woolfe getting out of a shiny black Audi. She wore a forest green flutter-sleeved kimono top with cropped sailor-front jeans and gold sandals.

"It's a divine creation from the new Tommy Hilfiger collection, and the color is so *magnifique* with her flowing red tresses and fair dewy skin," Avalon sighed, doing her best impression of a red-carpet fashion commentator.

"*Absolument,*" Halley agreed, getting into character herself. "And *j'adore* the way her hair is done, but not *over*done, which is so hard to do."

"*Bon* call!" Avalon said, tossing her straight blond locks dramatically.

"Hey, Cassidy." Halley smiled sweetly as the slender redhead approached. They'd never been friends, but they'd always been *friendly*.

"Cassidy! You must be so excited to start your term as Anna's vice-prez!" Avalon gushed, turning to walk with Cassidy toward the main building. "We were just talking about how amazing you look. Head-to-toe Tommy?"

"Yeah . . ." Cassidy's green eyes glinted. "You really know your stuff. You guys are looking pretty fab yourself. Who are you wearing?"

"Free People." Halley stopped walking and struck a head-back, hands-on-hips, pelvic-tilt pose to show off her deep plum bohemian dress over sparkle-black tights, which she'd paired with spruce-colored wedges. After the power breakfast and *major* mutual admiration over their second-day ensembles that morning, Avalon had tried to talk her out of the tights, but there was no point; the outfit would be nothing without them.

"Isaac," Avalon said, spinning around with one arm overhead. She slowly ran her other arm down her pink-checked minidress in *ta-da* mode. "But *not* from Tar-jay!" she added.

"*Of course not!*" Cassidy gasped, looking genuinely disturbed.

"We're totally going to Yes you," Avalon said with an excited shake. Halley nodded in agreement as the trio pushed through the lobby doors, heading for their lockers.

21

A few yards back, several eighth-grade boys were pretending not to watch them without much success.

"What do you mean?" Cassidy tilted her head. The only way she could look more angelic was if she had wings.

"Oh," Halley said. "You didn't hear about our column in the *Daily* competition?"

"No," Cassidy said earnestly.

"You've *got* to check it out," Halley said, stopping midway down a bank of gold lockers. "Especially since we'll be raving about you in tomorrow's fashion write-up."

"Wow. Okay . . . thanks!"

"That's one vote." Avalon smiled at Halley as Cassidy walked away. "And she's *such* a club-aholic. She'll totally get the Film Club, the Hiking Club, the Student Council, *and* the Knitting Society to vote for us, too."

"Hal!"

At the sound of her name, Halley turned away from Avalon. Sofee had just walked through the door from the arts quad with a guy she'd never seen before. A *cute* guy. Seriously cute.

"Hey, you." Sofee walked directly over to Halley and gave her a huge hug. "How's it going?"

"Great!" Halley grinned, trying to keep her heavily lashed blue eyes on Sofee and the row of gold lockers behind her. She didn't want to stare at the guy, but she didn't want to look like she was *trying* not to stare at him either. So she just focused on the silver R-O-C-K on Sofee's tight black camisole.

"Do you know Wade Houston?" Sofee asked as it dawned on Halley she was reading the four-letter word on Sofee's chest like it was the new issue of *Vogue*. Meaning, of course, that she was staring.

Halley glanced up, grateful for the go-ahead to look at the guy. Wade had messy black hair, so-dark-they-were-almost-black eyes with thick lashes, and full—but not *too* full—lips.

"Hey," Wade said, staring directly into Halley's eyes as he gave a casual wave.

"Hey." Halley cleared her throat in an attempt to cover up the fact that her voice had just cracked. "Are you new here?"

"Yeah." Wade ran a hand through his adorable fauxhawk, his eyes remaining locked with Halley's. "I just moved down from San Francisco a couple weeks ago."

"Oh, cool! Sofee and I were just in Berkeley for camp." She started to point to where Sofee had been standing but realized she wasn't there anymore. It was like the whole world had just fallen away and she and Wade were in their own bubble.

"I know," Wade said, like it was the most natural thing in the world for him to know all about Halley's life. Like he'd asked about her. Was that possible? Halley reminded herself to breathe. "I hear you had a phenomenal time."

Halley contemplated how to make Wade want to hear even *more* about her. But Wade's gaze had shifted to the gold lockers behind her—or more accurately, to the two girls in front of the lockers. So much for the bubble.

"You'll really like our column." Avalon was saying to Sofee. Her voice was all sweetness, but Halley knew it was an act. It sometimes surprised her that no one else saw through Avalon. "I think you'll get a lot out of it."

"Oh, you think?" Sofee replied with a laugh. "I don't think I need fashion advice from someone wearing a midget's dress."

"Um, it's actually Isaac," Avalon scoffed. "Isaac *Mizrahi*. I bought it at the Rack this summer, thank you very much."

"Oh, is that store named after you?" Sofee asked, fake-sincerely, glaring at Avalon's chest.

Halley stifled a laugh. She knew she should probably intervene, but some sort of magnetic force kept drawing her gaze back to Wade, who just smiled and raised his dark eyebrows at her. There was a tiny little freckle at the end of the left one. Or was it a mole? It looked like an exclamation point. Or maybe a question mark?

Halley felt like her head had been filled with helium. She looked over at Avalon, hoping she'd witnessed the seriously meaningful moment between Halley and the most amazing guy on the planet, but Avalon's eyes just widened in horror.

24

"Halley?" Avalon said through clenched teeth. "Are you just going to stand there?"

"Oh, please," Sofee spat. "I read your column this morning. It seems like *someone* can dish it but can't take it."

Halley was pretty sure that both her friends expected her to say something. But all she could think about was how Wade's hand would feel holding hers, walking down the hall, laughing at a hilarious inside joke. As she looked from Sofee's smug grin to Avalon's narrowed eyes to Wade's slim-fit black T-shirt, Halley realized that she didn't even care what they were arguing about.

"Um, Halley?" Sofee prodded.

"Yeah, Halley?" Avalon demanded.

Halley just smiled. She was wearing an adorable outfit, she'd met the perfect boy, and at least her two friends were talking. Um, right?

A total bust

"It's not working." Avalon frowned, turning to look at herself from another angle in the wall-to-wall mirrors of the girls' locker room. She pulled her hair into a ponytail and backed up to get a different view of her brand-new gymnastics leotard.

"Yes, it is." Halley grabbed an elastic so she could tie her hair back, too. "Seriously, you look rad. *Super*-rad. I'd kill to have boobs that weren't made by Victoria's Secret." She gave her lightly-padded bra a friendly pat.

Avalon didn't believe Halley for a second. After all, she had already referred to Avalon's boobs as "the *women*," and she didn't even stand up for her this morning. Avalon had no idea what was going on between her in front of Sofee and Halley, but she didn't want to think about it, let alone *talk* about it, now. She was sure that Halley was going to apologize any second, but all she could focus on was that *two* Nike Dri-FIT bras couldn't hide the fact that she was busting out all over.

"Once you get into your routine, you'll forget they're even there," Halley reassured her.

Yeah, right. Avalon gave her reflection one last sigh before walking over to the line of bright blue lockers, grabbing an oversize hoodie, and covering up her entire gymnastics leotard beneath it. Halley just shrugged and applied a coat of clear gloss to the model-perfect lips that matched her model-skinny body and her annoyingly cerulean blue eyes.

"Hey, Avalon!" Brianna stood at the end of the row of lockers, holding a stack of yellow flyers. "I'm glad I found you. Remember I told you Amy Channing dropped off the squad a few weeks ago?"

"Uh-huh." Avalon watched Halley put her lip gloss into her gym bag.

"Well, we have to replace her." Brianna held up one of her flyers. CHEERLEADING TRYOUTS THURSDAY—ONE SPOT OPEN. "So I've got to post these everywhere. Spread the word, 'kay?" Brianna began to flyer the locker room.

"Sure." Avalon smiled and turned to see the gymnastics coach walking in. Barely five feet tall, Coach Howe was still in Olympic-trials shape, and her ribs were threatening to poke through the long-sleeved white leotard she'd paired with navy-blue warm-up pants.

"Hey, Coach," Avalon said, heading over to grab her wristbands out of her own locker, right next to Halley's.

"Hi, Avalon. I'll see you girls out there. Thanks, Halley!" Coach Howe gave them each a pat on the shoulder as she bounced out to the gym carrying a Dominique Moceanu bobblehead, the tiny gold medalist nodding menacingly.

Avalon noticed a camcorder in Halley's hands, and before she could remember that she was mad at Halley and didn't want to talk to her, she was asking her what it was for.

"Coach made me the team's official videographer!" Halley announced. "She asked me to record all of today's routines so we can critique them at tomorrow's practice."

"Great." Avalon frowned. "Can't wait to see how the camera adds ten pounds to my already-enormo chest."

"Oh, please." Halley rolled her eyes and shook her head as she grabbed a tan sweatshirt and shut her locker.

"Where did you get your leotard?" interrupted Kimberleigh Weintraub—a tall, skinny girl with a long canary-yellow braid and a thick roll of bangs on her forehead—who was doing some standing stretches a few lockers down and extending her long pale arms overhead as she gazed approvingly at Halley.

While virtually every member of the gymnastics team opted to wear the standard Adidas practice ensemble in SMS's colors of royal blue with gold stripes, Avalon and Halley realized the importance of fashion, even in an athletic setting—

hence their new camouflage leotards: Halley's in classic khaki colors and Avalon's in three different shades of blue.

"GK Elite Sportswear," Halley replied. "It's where all the best Olympic gymnasts get their stuff."

"It's rad," Kimberleigh said, flaring her nostrils—which was her favorite facial expression for indicating enthusiasm. Kimberleigh's nose was already so upturned, Halley and Avalon generally referred to her as Piggleigh Swinetraub. "And I like your hoodie, Avalon."

"Thanks." Avalon smiled, pulling the zipper on her Hard Tail sweatshirt up even higher.

"You really do look amazing, Av," Brianna said. She handed a flyer to Halley, who sneered at it. "I've been telling you so all summer."

"Thanks, Bree." Avalon wanted to believe her, but she just felt so . . . noticeable. And not in the way she was used to. It seemed like there was a spotlight shining right on her chest all the time now. She said good-bye to Brianna, then unzipped her hoodie and looked down doubtfully.

"What is she?" Halley snickered when Brianna was out of earshot. "Your new *breast* friend?"

Avalon slammed the door to her locker with a loud *whack*. What was Halley's *problem*? "How about you get back to me after you've actually gone through puberty."

Halley didn't even respond, but Avalon saw her eyes go cold. She turned and stormed toward the door to the gym.

"Halley!" Avalon tried to catch up to her.

But as Avalon quickened her pace, she couldn't decide what was upsetting her most. Was it that:

1. She'd just intentionally hurt her best friend,
2. Her boobs were practically choreographing their own gymnastics routine beneath her leotard, or . . .
3. Halley had been the one to tease her *first*?

Avalon rezipped her hoodie and decided to put the answer on hold. For now, anyway.

The calm before the storm

The drive home had been tense. Halley just sat in the backseat and pretended to listen to her iPod while Avalon talked Abigail's ear off in the front. Halley would have to thank her mom for running interference—except then she might ask what was wrong. And Halley wouldn't know what to say.

What *was* wrong? Halley wondered as she poured herself a bowl of cereal with rice milk, her favorite post-gymnastics snack. Avalon had snapped at her out of nowhere and then didn't even apologize. Right after Halley had tried to make her feel better by assuring her she'd look great on camera!

"Wanna play Tekken?"

Halley looked up and saw her fifteen-year-old brother, Tyler, standing in the doorway of the kitchen.

"No, thanks," she said, barely even registering his sad

excuse for an outfit. She had attempted to give Tyler an extreme makeover on more than one occasion, but he always reverted back to the "before" picture within twenty-four hours.

"Wait, let me rephrase that: Come play Tekken with me or else . . ."

"Seriously, Tyler, I'm not in the mood to kick your butt in Tekken *again*. I've had a rough day." She slumped against the white marble countertop.

He laughed. "Oh, yeah. Second day of eighth grade is soooo awful."

Halley knew he wasn't trying to be mean—he was just being Tyler—but it still made her feel bad. She gathered her stuff and made her way past the shiny stainless-steel Viking stove and Sub-Zero fridge, giving Tyler a shove into the swinging metal-framed smoked-glass door to the living room as she walked past him.

"Oh, come on, Hal, I was kidding!" He started to pull on her Brooklyn Industries messenger bag, but she turned to glare at him. "Fine," he said. "Go sulk in your room. You're no fun."

When Halley got upstairs and closed her door, she felt better instantly. Her bedroom was the picture of modern bohemian hipness. She hadn't totally planned it that way, but somehow that's how it had evolved—from the tan suede beanbag in the corner to the white bedspread with big orange, turquoise, and yellow circles to the white egg-shaped desk chair with the cushy orange velvet cushion. Three shaggy throw rugs on the hardwood floor matched the circles on her bedspread perfectly, although the orange one was a bit more worn since Halley sat on it the most. Miscellaneous pages from *Vogue, InStyle, W,* and *Lucky* were taped directly to her cappuccino-colored walls.

Halley headed immediately for the sliding-glass doors that led out to a small gray stone patio and overlooked the back-yard below. From there, she had a clear view of the Greenes' palatial yellow Spanish-style house and the arched picture window of Avalon's bedroom. But instead of going outside, Halley quickly pulled down her taupe Roman shades so no one could see into her room.

Next she pushed all thoughts of Avalon out of her mind and instead focused on the *good* part of the day: meeting her soul mate, Wade. She fished her sketchpad out from under her bed, took a seat on her favorite orange rug, and opened her lime-green leather-bound scrapbook. She flipped through the pages, glancing at sketch after sketch: dolphins leaping above the waves . . . a dress she'd dreamed about one night . . . a surfboard . . . Avalon at the Cove . . . a harbor seal . . . Pucci . . . a Torrey Pines hiking trail . . . a little black skirt . . . a pair of aviator sunglasses . . . Then she began drawing her latest obsession—Wade. Halley exhaled deeply, drinking in every detail of the picture in her mind: his soft hair in the slightest hint of a fauxhawk, those intensely piercing eyes and insane lashes, the high cheekbones, the square chin . . .

As she drew the lines of his perfect, beautiful face, humming to herself as the picture started to take shape, she was sure that everything with Avalon would be fine eventually. Avalon would come over later and apologize, and they'd take Pucci on a walk. By tomorrow morning's ride to school, all the weirdness would be washed away and everything would be back to normal.

Right?

Girl, interrupted

*A*valon walked through the Brandons' rear sliding-glass doors and into their sparkling-white gourmet kitchen as if it were her own. Late-afternoon sunlight streamed through the floor-to-ceiling windows, dancing like fireflies on the hardwood floors. Avalon loved the Brandons' house. It was so comfortable and beachy, and she especially adored the gleaming white marble fireplace—perfect for making s'mores with Halley on chilly, fifty-degree winter evenings.

Avalon started upstairs to Halley's room with Pucci panting at her heels. Suddenly, two tattered black Vans slip-ons blocked her path. Her eyes trailed up to an equally unfortunate pair of faded Levi's. A T-shirt featuring Homer Simpson and the words SUGAR DADDY topped off Tyler Brandon's attempt at a high school uniform.

"Did Homer have pizza for lunch today?" Avalon asked,

wrinkling her nose at a greasy red splotch near the cartoon's yellow face.

"Ha-ha," Halley's brother fake-laughed. He grabbed the shiny silver banisters on either side of him, blocking the entire width of the stairway.

Aside from his perpetual state of fashion emergency and a mild case of video game–induced pallor, Tyler was actually geeky-cute. In fact, with their wavy brown hair, blue eyes, and light dusting of freckles, he and Halley kind of looked like twins.

"Is Hal in her room?"

"*Yesss!*" Tyler bellowed in his most ominous voice, arching his eyebrows so they nearly touched the dark crescent of hair flopping down over his forehead. "But if you want to pass, you must first pay the toll."

"Which is?" Avalon sighed, fighting back an amused smile at Tyler's severe dorkitude.

"Five rounds of Tekken," Tyler announced. "Get ready for the next battle!"

"Ohmygod, *move.*" Avalon rolled her eyes and pushed Tyler out of the way so she and Pucci could finally make their way up to Halley's room.

"You're no fun either!" he yelled after her.

She didn't have time for whatever Tyler was talking about. She was on a mission: to quickly resolve any awkwardness from what should have been a fine day at school and talk *parties*—specifically Friendapalooza, to which Avalon's mom had given the tentative green light. Now she just needed to convince Halley to get Mom Number Two on board and run tomorrow's Style Snarks column by Halley for her approval.

When Avalon got to the end of the hallway and cracked open Halley's door, she quickly stuck out her leg to block Pucci from rushing in. Halley's voice got raspy and soulful as she sang what sounded like an old Christina Aguilera ballad. But Avalon was pretty sure those weren't the "Beautiful" lyrics she remembered. Avalon leaned in closer.

"Oh, Wade, you're beautiful, so beautiful today.
I'm stoked you moved to town . . .
Yes, Wade, you're beautiful in every single way.
So glad we finally found . . .
. . . all of the love we found today."

Ohmygod. Halley was sitting on that ratty orange rug, hunched over a scrapbook, her charcoal and pencils strewn all around her. She wasn't just singing about this Wade guy. She was also . . . drawing *a sketch of him*? Avalon thought about closing the door quietly and then knocking on it loudly, as if she'd just arrived, but Pucci blew that plan by pushing past her leg and bounding into the room.

"Oh! Hey!" Halley's face went chalk-white, and she quickly closed her lime-green scrapbook.

"Hey," Avalon said, an embarrassed smile playing on her mouth. She focused on Halley's white egg-shaped desk chair, forcing herself not to laugh. "Um . . . uh . . . I was coming over to talk to you about Friendapalooza, but—" She stopped, thinking maybe this was exactly what they needed to break the ice, something they could joke about. "Apparently you're already having a . . . *party of your own!*" Avalon couldn't help but squeal the last few words.

"I was just working on a sketch." Halley kicked at the tan suede beanbag that Pucci sometimes slept on.

"Of a seriously *sketchy* guy." Avalon giggled. "Isn't that the freak Sofee was hanging with before school today?"

Halley whipped her head around. "He's not a freak."

"Oh, I'm sorry." Halley was joking, right? Avalon took a deep breath and squared her shoulders, feigning seriousness. "Do you have *feelings* for him?"

"The only *feeling* I have"—Halley gathered her drawing pencils and dropped them into a Hello Kitty pencil case— "is that your boobs have eaten your brain. Maybe Sofee was right about you."

Halley wasn't joking.

Avalon was stung by the first part of Halley's attack, but it was the second part that stopped her in her tracks. "What do you mean? What did *Softee* say about me?"

"Don't call her that," Halley said through clenched teeth.

"So you stick up for her even when she isn't here? But when she insults me, you just *laugh*? What *happened* to you over the summer?" Avalon demanded. "I mean, I was willing to overlook the lavender cowboy boots that scream, 'Yee-haw! Better not take my fashion advice, y'all!' But . . . I feel like I don't even *know* you anymore."

"And *I* don't understand how we were even friends in the first place!"

Avalon turned and ran. She was *not* going to give Halley the satisfaction of seeing her cry. She flew down the stairs and out the back door, then kept on running. It wasn't until she was back home, safe in the comfort of her own room that she allowed the tears to fall.

What had just happened? Avalon tugged at a lock of her blond hair and gazed out at the old oak tree growing near the sun-bleached fence that divided her backyard from Halley's. The trunk of the tree still had the girls' initials carved into it with the letters *B.S.* for "blood sisters," commemorating the day in kindergarten that they'd made their BFF bond official. But now, Avalon wished she could take a saw to that stupid tree. Who was this girl who had come back from art camp? For the first time in her life, Avalon was convinced that the Halley living next door was definitely *not* her best friend.

Style Stakeout

by the Style Snark—not Snarks

posted: wednesday, 9/10, at 7:01 a.m.

Since imitation is the sincerest form of flattery, it's a huge compliment that so many of you are already taking your style cues from my column—*and* my closet. I've never seen fashion roadkill cleaned up so quickly (buh-bye, tie-dye!), and I am *loving* the many ways you're incorporating the advice into your ensembles (hello, leopard-print footwear!). Of course, while some of you are already way ahead of the curve when it comes to trendsetting (big props to Cassidy on yesterday's *incredible* ensemble—a total YES!), others are desperately begging for help (sorry, Wynter, but your little brother wants his pirate costume back). That's why I've decided to devote today's special *solo* column to answering a few quick questions from our already-devoted readers:

Q: I've got this friend, but she's a total fashion NO. Should I avoid her until she starts dressing better?

A: YES. If you associate with a fashion NO, you're a NO-by-association.

Q: I'm a little bit top-heavy. Should I wear clothes that conceal that fact?
A: NO! If you've got it, flaunt it.

Q: Does my butt look big in this pink denim mini?
A: MAYBE. How much junk do you have in the trunk and how tight is the skirt?

That's it for today, dear readers. See you tomorrow, bright and early, with your one and only must-read style guide.

Shop on,
Avalon Greene

COMMENTS (118)

I just ordered a pair of leopard high-tops. So stoked. But where's Halley?
posted by writeon **on 9/10 at 7:22 a.m.**

OMG! U R so right about flaunting it if you've got it. I know I do . . . hee hee. ☺
posted by madameprez **on 9/10 at 7:37 a.m.**

Seriously? Who reads this column? David's Playlist is going to rock this competition!

posted by jimisghost **on 9/10 at 7:41 a.m.**

You go, girl. Great advice! Where's Halley this a.m.? Getting gorgeous, no doubt!

posted by cheeriously **on 9/10 at 7:43 a.m.**

Delusions of grandeur much? Some of us already know how to dress and don't need a column to tell us. And I hope Wynter makes you walk the plank for what you said. I thought she looked cute. I bet Halley would have something to say about that.

posted by surfergirl **on 9/10 at 7:56 a.m.**

BFFs are so last season

"Finally," Halley muttered under her breath as she emerged from Constance Greene's silver BMW. She waved a quick good-bye to Avalon's mom and gave Pucci a peck on top of her head before bolting from the car. She would have asked her parents to give her a ride instead, but they'd left ridiculously early for their beach yoga class.

Halley had almost made it to the glass doors of the school lobby when she heard the grating *slap-slap-slap* of Avalon's sandals on the red brick pathway behind her.

"Halley! Wait up!"

Halley slowly turned around. Maybe Avalon was going to apologize for completely insulting Halley's taste in clothes—and guys.

Avalon set her shoulders back, making her already generous chest look even more . . . charitable. She glared at Halley.

Then again, maybe she just wanted to pick up where she'd left off.

"What?" Halley asked, looking anywhere but directly at Avalon.

Avalon quickly unzipped her red patent leather tote bag and pulled out two bright orange folders, handing one to Halley. "I've outlined the terms of the dissolution of our relationship."

Halley choked as a laugh and a gasp met in her throat. "You've *got* to be kidding."

"Nope," Avalon said tersely. "And just so we're on the same page, I think we should go through it point-by-point right now."

Halley looked down at the folder in her hand, labeled GREENE-BRANDON SETTLEMENT AGREEMENT. She opened the folder, curious to see what Avalon had put in a document to which Halley had definitely not yet *agreed*.

"Okay, paragraph one: Property," Avalon read from her copy. "I've already boxed up a bunch of your stuff and left it on your back patio. You can get my things back to me whenever. I don't want to make a major deal out of it, but I do think you have at least three of my glitter pens and eight of my vintage *Vogue*s, and a bunch of clothes you don't even like or wear. So if you could return all that ASAP, that'd be great."

"Okay." Halley looked at Avalon and yawned in her face.

Avalon had always taken after her lawyer parents, but this was a little much, even for her.

"Great." Avalon cocked her head and flashed one of her big, toothy-white, I'm-just-pretending-to-be-happy smiles. "Paragraph two: School Grounds. You can take the front row, far-left desk in each of our classes, and I'll take the same row, far-right. Between periods, you can hang out on the east quad, and I'll hang in the lobby or in the garden." Avalon adjusted the cuffs of her shirt.

"No way!" Halley couldn't give up the Garden of Serenity. It was the best spot on campus!

"No way *what*?"

"I'll take the garden . . . you can have the east quad and the lobby," Halley negotiated, forgetting that she thought this whole thing was ridiculous.

"Whatever." Avalon exhaled so hard, Halley could smell her raspberry Bubble Yum breath. She made a few notes on her document with a squeaky red pen and kept reading. "Paragraph three: Extracurriculars. You can keep gymnastics this quarter, and we'll figure out our other sports if and when we go out for the teams."

"You're giving up gymnastics?" They'd been doing gymnastics together forever—and Avalon had rocked her floor routine yesterday, even if her boobs had bounced around more than she had. "But you *love* gymnastics."

"Um . . . I think I can survive without a balance beam."

Avalon fanned herself with her folder so her blond locks blew gently away from her face. She shuffled her gold sandal against the brick walkway. "Paragraph four: Social Life. You'll notice there are a few terms here, including division of friends. But I'd mostly like to talk about the Friendapalooza clause, wherein *I* will be having the party on my own."

"Wait." Halley cleared her throat and shifted the strap of her gray calfskin messenger bag on her shoulder. She was too dumbfounded to laugh. "So you still want to have a party celebrating our friendship when there's nothing left to celebrate?"

The Debatables, or at least the three unfortunates who represented the perfectly named debate team, had set up a bake sale next to the lobby entrance and were definitely eavesdropping. Halley shot them a look.

"Of course." Avalon nodded. "I'll just change the name to the Greene Party or something. Maybe mix it in with an eco-friendly fashion theme. Don't worry, I'll work out the details."

"I'm sure you will." Halley did her best to remain aloof, since she had no interest in the party anyway. "But who are you going to invite? The three friends you just gave your-self in this pathetic *agreement* to which I have in no way *agreed*?"

"Um, wrong. Those are just examples," Avalon sneered,

rolling her eyes up at the domed roof of the SMS entrance. "Besides, I'm inviting . . . the whole cheerleading squad!"

"Ohmygod, *yay!*" Halley squealed exaggeratedly, throwing her arms up in a V-for-victory pose. Avalon could have all the parties she wanted with her overly peppy friends—and the fact that she even thought Halley would care about missing out on her little bimbo-bash was beyond tragic.

"Great. So . . . paragraph five: Pet Custody." Avalon took one hand off the tote bag she'd been holding as a makeshift clipboard to tug at a lock of her hair.

Pet custody? Avalon hadn't even *wanted* Pucci at first. She'd tried to convince Halley to beg for a puggle.

"You take Pucci every Monday, Tuesday, Thursday, and alternating Fridays," Avalon was saying. "I'll have her on all the other days."

"But that means you get to spend more time with her because I only have her on school days and you have her all weekend," Halley pointed out as her stomach dropped. First Avalon thought she could take the Garden of Serenity . . . and now the *puppy?*

"I did consider that, but honestly? You're lucky I'm not asking for sole custody." Avalon took a deep breath before continuing. "I mean, I took care of her all summer—and those were the most formative months of her life. Plus, your disorganized lifestyle really isn't conducive to caring for Pucci. She *is* just a puppy, and let's face it: You're a bad influence and pretty much an unfit pet parent."

Someone at the Debatables bake sale gasped.

"This is ridiculous." Halley turned toward the lobby doors as the warning bell for first period rang. She didn't care what Avalon had put in her sorry excuse for an agreement; she wasn't going to let anybody tell her where she could go or when she could see her dog.

"Hang on!" Avalon said, lightly grabbing Halley's tanned arm, which Halley immediately pulled away. "We just have one more item: the *Daily* column competition."

Halley had no interest in hearing any more. She walked through the lobby, pushing past her startled classmates, ready to tear up Avalon's contract and throw the pieces of paper back in her face.

"I'll enter the competition on my own, since I'm obviously more of a fashion authority than you, and since today's column is going over so well," Avalon called after Halley.

When Halley got to the exit on the other side of the lobby, she glanced down at her copy of the agreement:

AVALON GREENE WILL HERETOFORE IRREVOCABLY ASSUME RESPONSIBILITY FOR THE COLUMN COMPETITION SINCE SHE IS BETTER VERSED IN FASHION AND IS THE MASTER-MIND BEHIND STYLE SNARKS.

"Wrong . . . and wrong!" Halley called back when she read the words.

"Excuse me?" Avalon had caught up to her along the brick footpath to journalism class.

"You *think* you know fashion, but you *don't*," Halley snapped, stopping short so Avalon bumped into her. It was bad enough that Avalon had completely edited their column this morning and submitted it without Halley's name, but did she have to give the whole school such silly advice, too?

"And you think *you* know fashion?" Avalon shot back, scowling at Halley's beige Lux sweetheart top, which she'd paired with a brown knee-length pencil skirt and button-up booties.

"Obviously." Halley eyed the snug navy tank Avalon was wearing to illustrate her new tighter-is-better philosophy. If anyone had slipped on the style meter, it was Avalon. She was probably just bitter that she'd so obviously lost her fashion edge.

"Yeah, right." Avalon tossed her head and started walking up the footpath again. "The column was my idea. And I'm *not* giving it up."

"No, it wasn't, and neither am I."

"Then we'll split it." Avalon quickened her pace.

"How?" Halley asked, now trying to catch up to Avalon as they neared the journalism villa.

"I'll write tomorrow's, you can write Friday's, and then

we'll just alternate them till the end of the competition," Avalon said. "When people vote, they can say which one of us they like better."

"Fine!" Halley shouted over the first-period bell.

"Fine!" Avalon shouted back, throwing open the classroom door. "And may the best Snark win."

"Oh, *I will!*" Halley stormed to a desk in the back of the villa, despite Avalon's agreement confining her to the front-row, far-left desk. She couldn't wait to do to Avalon's column what Avalon had done to their friendship: destroy it.

Turning the tables

As Avalon carried her lunch tray past her classmates, she felt like she was in one of those dreams where you look down and realize you're naked. But she was fully clothed, in a super-cute navy tank and plaid Bermuda shorts, no less. So why did she feel so . . . exposed? She swallowed hard, squared her shoulders, and focused on the smoked-glass doors leading from the dining hall to the covered outdoor terrace.

Slap, slap, slap.

Avalon was soothed by the sound her gold sandals made as she walked along the shiny marble floor.

"Hey, Avalon!" came a familiar voice from behind her.

"Bree." Avalon turned to smile at her friend.

"How's it going?" Brianna asked, looking at Avalon's tray. "Hey! We both got the seared ahi."

"I know . . . yum, right?" Avalon smiled as she and Brianna walked out onto the terrace. She tried not to stare at the table she and Halley had shared for the past two years, but Halley was already there, surrounded by Anna, Lizbeth, and Carrie.

"Avalon!" Halley shouted. Avalon kept walking, thinking she could pretend she hadn't heard, but Halley shouted her name again, giving Avalon no choice but to acknowledge her. "Can you come here?"

Avalon tried to smile as she shuffled closer to her ex–best friend. What could she possibly want?

Halley set her white linen napkin down on the glass table-top and glanced at the girls sitting on either side of her. "So, is it okay I'm sitting here?" A smirk played on Halley's lips.

"Sure." Avalon nodded, tightening her grip on her lunch tray. "Why?"

"Well . . ." Halley leaned down and pulled the orange folder from her messenger bag. "Paragraph two of your agreement didn't address the division of the dining hall, so I was really freaking out about where I was allowed to sit without getting hauled off to juvie or something!"

Avalon rolled her eyes. *How immature.*

She'd simply wanted to make things easier on *both* of them—but she wasn't exactly surprised Halley was being so snotty and childish about it.

"So anyway, could you send over the paperwork and I'll

have my people take a look and get back to you?" Halley laughed while Anna, Carrie, and Lizbeth awkwardly stared down at their plates.

"Um . . . okay." Avalon gave Halley a sideways look, feeling a surge of power when their audience ignored the attempted jab. Then she tossed a quick smile at Brianna and continued: "Oh, look, there's the squad! Let's go." Avalon gestured to the table where the cheerleaders always sat, deciding her victory was complete when Halley's jaw dropped. "Later, guys . . . *bon appétit!*"

"What was *that* about?" Brianna asked as she and Avalon walked over to the cheer table.

"Nothing major." Avalon wasn't sure what she should tell people. What was Halley telling everybody? She pasted on her most convincing smile and said, "Halley and I just figured it was time to do some things separately—you know, carve out our own identities?"

"Oh." Brianna nodded sagely. Avalon could tell she didn't need to explain things any further. Brianna *obviously* understood.

"Speaking of," Avalon moved on with a sly grin, "is that spot on the pep squad still open? I'm kind of over gymnastics."

"Ohmygod! Really?" Brianna nearly dropped her tray. "Yes! Tryouts are tomorrow at three-thirty!"

Avalon knew exactly when tryouts were. She'd been

53

mentally practicing her moves ever since drafting the settlement last night. It's not that she wasn't bummed to give up gymnastics, because she most definitely was. She was good at gymnastics—better than Halley—but with her new . . . developments, she knew it was no longer the right sport for her. Better to join a team where her assets wouldn't hold her back.

As she sat down at the cheer table and said hello to everyone, Avalon raised her glass of Pellegrino and silently toasted herself: *To new beginnings.*

The art of war

"Hey, that's really good."

Halley swiveled around on her black vinyl–cushioned stool. Sofee had been watching her put the finishing touches on her charcoal assignment as the final bell rang.

"Oh, thanks." Halley grinned. "Trees are my specialty." Halley slid the charcoal weeping willow sketch to one side of the large white drafting table and tore out a fresh sheet of paper from her sketchbook, hoping to draw away the tiny bubble of stress that was beginning to float around her head.

"I know." Sofee nodded, wrapping her iPod earbuds around her tiny red Nano. Clad in one of her classic ensembles—dark skinny pants and a slim-fit LONDON CALLING T-shirt with bright red high-top Chuck Taylors, Sofee stood out next to the art studio's tall white drafting tables. Normally Halley would have frowned on such a definable "look," but Sofee's long, wavy black-and-blond-streaked hair, freckle-size diamond nose ring, and perpetually tanned skin set her apart from the style-drones crowding the SMS hallway. "That mangled oak you did at camp rocked. Everybody thought so."

"Thanks." Halley sighed happily as she drew indigo-blue swirls and spirals on the edge of the page, then switched to a sunflower-yellow pencil and worked on an image in the middle—not yet sure what it would turn into. As she picked up several other pencils and blended them together, she quickly realized she'd created a new color: Pucci gold! She continued to draw, turning the picture into an amazing likeness of her and Avalon's beloved puppy.

"So, what have you been up to since we got back—besides school?" Sofee asked.

"Not much," Halley said, wondering how long she'd have to wait to "casually" ask Sofee about Wade, what his top ten interests were, and how long Sofee thought it would take to make him Halley's first boyfriend. "You know, just hanging. How 'bout you?"

"Well . . ." Sofee paused for a second. "I joined a band!"

"That's awesome!" Halley said, truly excited for her new friend.

Sofee had blown everyone away when she played a set of Coldplay, Blue October, and Snow Patrol songs at the end-of-camp bonfire. She had talked about wanting to start a band all summer. Halley was impressed that she'd already gone for it. But, then, Sofee wasn't one to sit around.

"I know, right?" Sofee opened the black military-style satchel with a red star on the flap that was slung across her torso and pulled out a show flyer, handing it to Halley. "We're called the Dead Romeos."

Halley looked at the flyer, which featured a hand-drawn picture of Sofee, a couple of other guys that looked vaguely familiar, and . . . *Wade*!

Halley smiled, trying to remain calm as she calculated her next question, first rehearsing it in her head, and then finally saying it out loud: "Is that the guy you introduced me to yesterday?"

Sofee nodded. "Uh-huh. He sings lead."

"That's cool. He seemed really nice."

"He is." Sofee grinned. "All the guys in the band are."

"I can't wait to hear you play," Halley enthused, putting her sketches into her calfskin bag and standing up to leave.

"You can be our fan club president or something!" Sofee laughed as they brushed past a line of easels and stools. Halley ran her hand along the supply wall—a series of different-size black bookcases with wire baskets full of every imaginable kind of paint, pencil, and pastel, as well as stacks of sketchbooks, metal palettes, and prestretched canvases—as they walked out of the classroom. The hallways were crowded with girls in knockoff versions of Halley's and Avalon's outfits from the day before. Even the guys looked like they were trying a little harder today.

"Totally." Halley giggled.

"Or maybe you can be . . . our *flyer-making publicist*?" Sofee raised her eyebrows hopefully at Halley, who looked down at the flyer in her hand. "I mean, I've been working on that thing since Monday, and it's just not getting any better."

"Well, it's not *bad*," Halley said honestly, examining Sofee's work. It was true that Sofee hadn't exactly captured Wade's perfection. The freckle next to his left eyebrow was totally missing, for starters. "But I can take a shot at it, if you want."

"Yes, *please*!" Sofee begged as they walked along a row of gold lockers. "You're so much better at sketching than I am."

"But you're going to be a *rock star*!" Halley squealed as they arrived at her locker near the SMS lobby.

Sofee glanced around tentatively as if she were looking for someone. Then she leaned in and whispered: "Know what I don't get?"

"What?" Halley asked, punching in her locker combination: *12-23-96*. It was Avalon's birthday. Her combination was Halley's.

"How can you be friends with *Avalon Greene*?" Sofee picked at a loose thread on the hem of her shirt. "I mean, I know you said she was cool, that I should give her a chance . . . but, well, I tried and I just don't get it." Sofee shrugged almost apologetically. "I mean, you're so rad and chill, and she's like this uptight Little Miss Perfect."

Halley fought the urge to defend her best friend—er, *former* best friend. Last week, Halley would have said that Avalon just had a unique charm. But now? For the first time, she kind of had to agree.

"Hmmm." Halley frowned as she closed her locker. "Maybe that's why we're not hanging out anymore."

"Really?" Sofee's dark eyes brightened instantly.

Halley nodded tentatively. It felt weird to say it out loud. She hadn't gone into the details with Carrie, Anna, and Lizbeth at lunch. She had just said that she and Avalon had had a disagreement, because she wasn't really sure *what* was happening.

Halley opened up her messenger bag to switch out her art notebook for her Earth Science folder. That's when she saw Avalon's lame orange folder full of friendship legalese. She was feeling totally off balance and knew it had everything to do with Avalon and that *ridiculous* agreement she'd thrown at her. Especially the part about Halley being an unfit pet parent. She took a deep breath and tried to convince herself she was entitled to bad-mouth her ex-BF. "Yeah. I mean, it's hard to hang out with someone *that* uptight, you know?"

"I know, right!" Sofee sounded so relieved. "Is she *always* that *obsessive*?"

"Yeah! It's so tragic," Halley said without thinking, the words tumbling out of her mouth. "I mean, would you believe she actually color-codes her underwear drawer—and puts expiration dates on each of the compartments so she doesn't have to deal with rotting elastic?"

"That's absurd!" Sofee laughed so hard, she had to wipe away a tear.

Halley giggled along with Sofee, but she felt queasy. Even though the story was true, it sounded so much worse than it really was. It was like she was in a game of tug-of-war—with her feelings for the old Avalon pulling her in one direction, and her disgust for the new Avalon pulling her in another. Before, Halley thought labeled underwear compartments were a good idea. But now, Halley was having fun mocking them. Before, Halley defended Avalon. Now, she spilled secrets she'd sworn on a stack of vintage *Vogues* never to tell anybody.

"Well, if you don't have plans with Avalon," Sofee started, "maybe you should come watch me and the band rehearse tomorrow after school. Get some inspiration for the flyer or something."

No sooner had the words slipped past Sofee's mauve-glossed lips than the fog lifted and Halley felt like herself again. A better, Avalon-free version of herself: relaxed, confident, and happy. Tomorrow she was going to see Wade, and maybe—just maybe—once they locked eyes, he'd tell her he wrote a brand-new song about how awesome she was.

"Sounds great." Halley smiled. It was the first genuine smile she'd had all day.

The official cyberzine of **Seaview Middle School**

SCHOOL NEWS | HEALTH | SPORTS | ENTERTAINMENT | **COMPETITION**

Out with the Old

by Style Snark A

posted: thursday, 9/11, at 7:21 a.m.

Hey, style mavens: Just a quick FYI to let you know the Snarks are now officially dividing our reporting duties—so you'll be getting each of us on alternating days, at least until you decide on the column competition winner (Vote for A! Vote for A! ☺). After the overwhelming response to my post yesterday, I just knew I had to give you another daily dose before handing over the baton.

It's quite fitting that we're splitting things in such a fashion. (No pun intended! Okay, maybe a little one.) After all, being on the cutting edge means adapting to change. Think about it: Why would you want to hold on to something that's unattractive, unappealing, or completely outdated? And how do you know when something's gotta go? Here are a few F-words for you:

1. **Was it just a FAD?** Leaping on the latest trend is an honest mistake. But if that trend is over faster than you can say

"button-up boots!"—which, let's be honest, were *always* a NO—just admit your bad and find a new fad. Better yet, try for something with more staying power next time.

2. **Is it majorly FREAKY?** You might have thought those sparkly tights were super-cute, but didn't the looks of terror on your friends' faces tell you to think again? They were a MAYBE at best, so for goodness' sake, *take them off and shred them*! (Maybe they'll come in handy for an art project!)

3. **Is it completely FORGOTTEN?** If you liked it when you first saw it, but never even thought about it after you brought it home, obviously it wasn't worth keeping. Translation: Pack up that depressing Camp Loser ensemble and ship it off to someone who will appreciate it (like a Salvation Army shopper).

So, to sum up: Keep moving Fashion-Forward and Forget about last season's Faux-pas. Every day is a Fresh chance to be Fabulous.

That's it for today, people. Just remember the F-words, and you'll be looking Fantastic.

Shop on,
Avalon Greene

So it's true? There's been a catfight on the catwalk! Did the Style Snarks completely break up? Either way, I am so loving the claws on this column.☺

posted by luv2gossip **on 9/11 at 7:28 a.m.**

Now we know who the real snark is . . . Style Snark A!

posted by superstyleme **on 9/11 at 7:45 a.m.**

Teamwork wins games, ladies. Any decent coach will tell you: This spells disaster!

posted by fourstrikes **on 9/11 at 7:49 a.m.**

Totally informative. I'm boxing up my hideous leadership camp clothes and ditching them right after school. Thank U.

posted by veepme **on 9/11 at 7:58 a.m.**

Something to cheer about

The afternoon sun beat down on Avalon as she marched past the SMS villas. It was only three-fifteen, but already she could hear voices chanting enthusiastically from the football field.

"Turn on the power, turn on the drive, fire it up, let's go!"

It was a painfully hot and humid afternoon, and the sun kept ducking behind the clouds, casting an eerie and depressingly muted glow over the campus. Avalon wiped the moisture from her forehead with the back of her hand. She took off her sage-green Roxy hoodie, which she'd paired with matching capris, a white sports tank, and white Nikes with a green stripe. She was dressed to impress and ready to rock cheerleading tryouts.

"Hey, Avalon!" Brianna called out from her spot in front of the bleachers, where ten hopefuls were already sitting nervously on the lowest bench. "Tryout forms are over there, and we're going to get started in a few minutes."

As Brianna jogged over to the squad, Avalon grabbed a form and a pen and quickly filled out the sheet. She put on her game face, smiling her hellos to a few of the girls on the bleachers as she joined them.

"All right!" Brianna bounced back over to the bleachers while the rest of the cheerleaders remained on the field, practicing their routines with Coach Carlson—a short, rotund, rosy-cheeked woman with frizzy orange hair and an unfortunate affection for all-American sweatshirts. Today's selection was bright red with short sleeves and an eagle carrying a U.S. flag in its beak emblazoned across the front. This was paired with electric blue shorts that were a bit too tight for her thick, pale legs.

"As you all know, our squad got cut down to nine girls since Amy Channing's dad was transferred to Chicago," Brianna said, focusing on Avalon before addressing the other contenders. "We really need ten girls to reach our optimum potential—and that's why you're all here. We're going to teach you a pretty basic cheer, and then you'll each get a chance to give it your best shot. For now, just stand behind the squad and watch a few run-throughs."

Avalon headed out to the football field with the rest of the group. She glanced at the girls next to her, who were putting on their peppiest faces. She was the obvious choice. Visions of cute cheerleading uniforms with AVALON embroidered on the chest danced in her head.

"Okay, everyone follow along!" Brianna yelled.

Avalon snapped back to attention. It was time to show the other girls just how stiff their competition was.

Brianna took a deep breath before yelling, "Ready? Okay!" and then she launched into the cheer.

Wait, what was the first line? Avalon attempted to keep up, but every time she tried to get the words right, her steps fell behind a beat. And what was *wrong* with her hand claps?

"Great job, ladies! Just a couple more run-throughs, and you'll have it!" Brianna's cheery voice sent a nervous trickle of sweat down Avalon's back.

Okay, focus. You can do this, Avalon told herself. Taking a deep breath, she made her arms as rigid as she could and willed herself to stay on beat.

This was harder than it looked. Avalon clapped so hard, her hands hurt. *Not making the squad isn't an option. You gave up gymnastics for this.* The little voice inside Avalon's head was beginning to drown out the cheer she was yelling at the top of her lungs. She glanced around her. At least the rest of the hopefuls seemed to be struggling, too. And she had Brianna on her side.

"All right, girls. Let's see what you've got!" Brianna gathered all the potential cheerleaders around her. "Grab a number from the bowl on the table. Number one, meet us on the field. Number two, you're on deck. Good luck, everyone!"

Avalon breathed a giant sigh of relief when she drew her tryout number: ten. Last. She jogged over to the bleachers. Avalon had never understood people who don't watch their competitors. She needed to know exactly which girls she had to beat.

There was:

1. Kitty Jenkins, who was really loud and had super-crisp moves, but Avalon was distracted by her dark-rimmed glasses and the massive, frizzy brown ponytail that repeatedly whipped Kitty in the face.

2. Laura Mortenson, with her long blond ponytail and sparkling blue eyes. She looked the part, but her deep, breathy voice sounded more Marilyn Monroe–intense than cheerleader-happy.

3. Ximena du Pont, who claimed to be from the du Pont dynasty, but really just adopted the name when her mom divorced her dad, the NFL coach. The one thing she *had* inherited was his physique.

As Avalon looked around the emerald-green field overlooking the Pacific Ocean, she decided that this was going to be easier than she expected. No one else even posed a threat.

By the time Brianna summoned her to the field, Avalon was ready.

She leapt up from her spot on the bleachers and ran out to the field. Coach Carlson and the entire squad were sitting at the table, pens in hand, ready to rate Avalon's performance.

"Whenever you're ready," Brianna yelled.

Avalon stood straight and rigid with her hands behind her back and smiled wider than she ever had in her life. She chased the last butterfly out of her stomach and took a deep breath.

Ready? OKAY!
L-I-O-N-S!
We're lions, we don't take no mess!
Lions, lions, hear us roar!
Lions, lions, watch us score!
Lions, lions, can't be beat!
Lions, get up off your feet!
Gooooo, Lions!

Avalon was so wrapped up in the moment that she didn't even pause before throwing in a quick back handspring. With a huge smile on her face, she slid down into the splits to seal the deal. "Go, Lions! Number one!"

"Great job!" Brianna smiled, glancing over at Coach Carlson, who offered a thumbs-up. A few cheerleaders at the table clapped and grinned. Kitty, Laura, and Ximena looked crestfallen. Avalon silently thanked every gymnastics coach she'd ever had.

"Okay, everyone." Brianna turned toward the bleachers as Avalon rejoined the other hopefuls and swallowed down the nervous lump in her throat. "Go ahead and hang out while we calculate your scores."

Brianna, Coach Carlson, and the rest of the cheerleaders huddled around the table.

"So, where's the other half of Halvalon?" asked Kitty, sidling up next to Avalon.

"Oh, she's sticking with gymnastics this semester," Avalon explained nonchalantly. "But I decided it was time for a change."

"Right on," Kitty said, taking off her glasses and cleaning them on her baby-pink tank top. A breeze rustled her puffy hair. "You did really well."

"Thanks! So did you," Avalon assured her.

"Your back handspring was awesome," Laura said softly, joining the conversation. "I bet you get the spot."

"We'll see . . . ," Avalon said, hoping Laura was right. "It *is* a lot like gymnastics, but way harder than I thought it would be."

"Totally harder!" agreed Justine Zimmermann, a petite brunette with asparagus-green eyes who was sitting to Avalon's left, scratching at a grass stain on her beige shorts. *She* didn't have a shot.

Avalon didn't have time to respond. The circle of cheer-leaders had broken up.

"Okay!" Brianna placed her hands on her hips and struck a wide-legged stance as if she were about to launch into a cheer. "We've calculated the scores, and it was really, really close. But, our new squad member is—" The cheerleaders ran into a V-formation.

"*A-V-A-L-O-N!* Avalon! Avalon! Avalon!"

"Ohmygod, you guys, thank you so much," Avalon practically screamed.

After Avalon joined her new team for a few long seconds of squealing and jumping up and down on the field, Coach Carlson called Brianna over to discuss uniforms. Avalon followed the rest of the squad back to the locker room. She breathed in the salty air and looked out at the waves crashing toward the cliffs. The grassy hills of the SMS campus seemed even greener today than usual.

"You did really well today. Congrats!" said the squad's co-captain, Sydney McDowell, as they headed inside. With purple terry-cloth Juicy shorts on her Tootsie Roll Midgee-esque legs and hoodie that matched her violet eyes, Sydney looked like a pigtailed grape. And though her words were nice, the expression on her face was not.

"Thanks." Avalon tried to ignore Sydney and focus instead on the fact that she was now a full-fledged *cheer-leader*. She was one of them. Hello, short skirts and tailored sweaters and cute football and baseball and water polo players!

"Hey, guys, didn't Avalon remind you of that herkie-jerky girl at camp?" Sydney asked the others as they all stood at their lockers.

The herkie-jerky girl? What is that *supposed to mean? It doesn't sound like a compliment. . . .*

"Hey, yeah, I totally forgot about her," replied Tanya Williams, her stretchy white vest and shorts accentuating her muscular Louis Vuitton–brown limbs.

"Oooh! And remember how her squad did that skit with the giant, scary-looking teddy bear?" chimed in Andi Lynch, a perky, curly-haired brunette who apparently felt the need to yell even when she was only a few inches away.

"Ugh, they were *so* lame." Sydney laughed, turning to face the rest of the squad. "They didn't even know the difference between a half-elevator and a full-elevator. And when they choked on the free liberty, herkie-jerky almost broke her leg!"

"Ohmygod! That was so seriously insane!" Andi squealed.

Avalon stared blankly into her locker as the girls giggled about cheer camp and last year's games and bus rides with the boys. She thought hanging out with Bree this summer would give her an in—but she'd never felt more *out*. There was so much to being a cheerleader that Avalon hadn't realized. She'd already come this far, though. And it wasn't like she could turn back now . . . even if she wanted to.

I'm with the band

Halley stood in the doorway of the music room, trying to time her entrance perfectly. Big silver notes were painted on the blue walls and all the furniture was musically themed. Most of the chairs looked like notes. She stared at the back of Wade's head and his shiny black hair, and then allowed her eyes to travel down to his faded navy T-shirt and a metal-studded brown leather belt. He was sitting at the black baby grand piano, playing a few keys that sounded like The Fray.

"Awesome!" A short, stocky boy with shaggy dirty-blond hair whom Halley hadn't spoken to since elementary school walked over to a set of sparkly royal-blue drums. He began tapping out a beat. What was his name? Mason *Something* . . . Halley's gaze went back to Wade's perfect, thick hair.

A lanky, freckly guy with wild, curly dark hair that hung past his earlobes picked up a maple-colored electric bass and added a steady, rhythmic groove. She couldn't remember his name at all. Halley crept in and sat in a folding metal chair near the door, watching as Sofee grabbed a cherry-red electric guitar and joined the jam session.

Halley was pretty sure her eyes did that cartoony red-hearts thing when Wade started singing. She couldn't make out all the words, but the song sounded like it had something to do with a girl and an ocean and a field of wheat. It was without question the best song Halley had ever heard.

"We rock!" Mason squealed when the song ended. He leapt up from behind his drums and accidentally tossed a stick in the air, sending it flying toward Halley. "What is *she* doing here?"

"Hey, you're here!" Sofee smiled, setting her guitar back against its metal stand and rushing over. "She's with me." Sofee practically dragged Halley toward the tiny stage at the front of the room. "I asked her to redo our flyers, since mine fully stunk."

"They were fine," Wade said, pivoting around on the piano bench and standing up.

Halley could finally see that perfect face, his deliciously juicy lips, that . . .

"But we can always use more flyers."

"Halley, you remember Wade?" Sofee asked, leading Halley

73

over to the piano. "And that's Evan Davidson and Mason Lawrence." Curly-haired Evan looked at his feet.

"Hey," Halley said, holding up one navy-blue-manicured hand. "That song was awesome."

"You think?" Mason looked at Halley with his head tilted.

"Uh-huh." Halley nodded confidently and wondered if Wade noticed that Mason seemed to like her. She was no expert on guys, but it was obvious the drummer was crushing on her. That was fine—all the better to make Wade jealous.

"Thanks." Wade beamed, fixing his dark eyes on Halley. He shifted around on the piano bench. *Score!* "We just started working on it, so it's just gonna get better."

"Hopefully . . . ," Evan said quietly, giving Halley a shy smile. He reminded her of a more serious version of her brother. "So, you like the Beastie Boys?"

Halley was glad *someone* in the band had noticed the T-shirt she'd snagged from her mom's closet specifically for her cameo at the Dead Romeos' rehearsal.

"Oh, yeah." Halley nodded, casually tossing her head so her hair fell in front of her right shoulder. She'd practiced the hair move about a million times since last night. Normally she would have asked Avalon to confirm that it looked as cool as she thought it did, but she was *nearly* certain it was totally irresistible. "My mom used to work in the music business and saw them in concert, like, a hundred times."

"Wow!" Evan pushed his dark hair out of his face, but

it just flopped back down. "What other bands did she know?"

"Ummm." Halley tried to remember the names of the artists on the plaques hanging in the Brandons' upstairs hallway. "Duran Duran, Crowded House, Red Hot Chili Peppers, R.E.M., the Beatles—?"

Mason dropped his remaining drumstick. "Your *mom* knew the *Beatles*? Aren't they all *dead*?"

Halley laughed like she knew something Mason didn't. She had no idea if her mom actually knew any of those bands, but figured she was close enough—for now, anyway. *Mental note: Listen to some of those boxed-up CDs in the garage.*

"Hey, why don't you stay for another song or two?" Wade suggested. "Maybe you can tell us what you think."

"Yeah, Halley. Stay," Sofee added with a strum of her guitar.

Halley smiled and sat down, leaning back against the note-chair. Mason retrieved his drumsticks and counted off the beginning of a song. Halley felt like she had tickets to the hottest concert in town, and the lead singer was going to invite her backstage to hang out *any minute now*.

Of course, Halley couldn't even pretend to listen to the words. It was like the band was playing backup for the duet of love that was clearly about to begin any moment now. And the longer the song went on, the more Wade seemed to be looking over at her.

By the time they were wrapping up their third song, Halley was woozy. She'd never been this excited before. Not even winning a gymnastics meet could top this feeling.

Ohmygod! Gymnastics!

Halley turned to look at the clock on the back wall of the music room. 3:48. She was eighteen minutes late for practice! She grabbed her messenger bag and rushed toward the door.

"Hey! Where you going?" Mason yelled after Halley.

"Oh—sorry!" Halley called back. "That was awesome. But I'm late—see you!"

Halley couldn't have planned a better exit from band rehearsal. It was *so* Cinderella. It would definitely add to her mystique. How could Wade possibly resist?

The hate is on

G ray Lexus SUV, yellow Hummer, green Jaguar convert-ible, white Prius, silver Beemer SUV, red Jeep, gold Kia Rio—ew! Kia? Avalon sighed as car after car pulled past the wrought-iron gates and around the grassy embankment in the center of the SMS circular driveway. She waved good-bye to some of her *former* gymnastics teammates and *current* fellow cheerleaders as they piled into their parents' cars.

It was a sweltering eighty-degree afternoon, and Halley and Avalon were both trying to take cover from the sun under the shady domed courtyard entrance while waiting for Abigail Brandon to pick them up. Avalon stole a quick glance over her right shoulder as Halley rifled through her brown leather messenger bag. She was obviously trying to look busy so she wouldn't have to interact with Avalon.

The one thing the girls hadn't been able to divide up: carpooling. Alas, none of the cars in the long line of vehicles belonged to Halley's mom—not that Avalon was looking forward to riding home with one Brandon, let alone two.

Avalon puffed out her lower lip and blew upward in a futile attempt to cool herself down. She wished she hadn't changed back into her gray cashmere vest after cheerleading tryouts. Her entire body felt prickly and sticky with sweat, and the current awkwardness between her and Halley made everything all the more uncomfortable. A sheet of paper blew toward Avalon's feet. Her eyes followed it along the ground. It looked like a drawing of Sofee Hughes and . . . that Wade guy Halley had been singing about. Was she still working on sketches of the sketchoid? Avalon bent down and grabbed the paper off the ground.

"Hey, that's what I was looking for," Halley said, trying to grab at the half-drawn flyer for the Dead Romeos. "Give it back!"

"Ohmygod, groupie much?" Avalon sneered, shoving the flyer at Halley.

"*Groupie?*" Halley grabbed the paper and clutched it as if it were one of the rare vintage copies of *Vogue* they'd scored for fifty dollars each on eBay. "Nice try, but I'm actually *friends* with the band, and I'm working on a new flyer for their show. In fact, I'm their *publicist!*"

Tragic! Avalon couldn't decide whether to be amused or

disturbed by Halley's new rocker-stalker status. "Well, hopefully you can draw a better picture of Sofee—and make her
as *hideous* as she is in real life!"

"Whatever." Halley slung her bag onto her shoulder, hurling a defensive glare at Avalon. "Sofee's gorgeous."

"Yeah, right." Avalon laughed loudly. Too loudly to be
convincing? "The girl is a poseur! And since you've apparently become a poseur wannabe, I guess that makes you—
what?—a pose-a-be?"

"Jealous much?" Halley shot back quickly, pulling at her
shirt in an attempt to create a body breeze and looking down
at the ground without much conviction.

"Oh, yeah, I'm *so* jealous of that emaciated little pierceaholic!"

"One tiny little nose ring doesn't make you a pierceaholic."
Halley squinted at Avalon. "And at least she's not a tanorexic
*bleach*aholic like you!"

"Excuse me? This is my *natural* color—from the *sun*,"
Avalon insisted, aggressively pulling at her ponytail with
both hands, which were beginning to shake as she twisted
it into a loose knot. She'd had professional highlights done
only twice, and she was positive the color had grown out.
"And tanorexic? Isn't that the pot calling the kettle tan?"

"This is my *natural* color—from the *sun*," Halley parroted
back mockingly, scrunching up her freckled nose. "You're
the one who goes from the beach to the pool to the spray

bottle . . . and I'm sure it'll just get worse now that you're BFFs with that girl from the *poop* squad!"

"Ohmygod, *poop* squad? That's so weak." Avalon sneered. "And please refrain from insulting the captain of *our* squad. I happen to be a cheerleader now, too!"

Halley's eyes widened with terror.

"I just made the team." Avalon tossed her head haughtily, but the announcement felt a little anticlimactic. Revealing her news in the middle of such a brutal insult-a-thon wasn't exactly what she'd been planning.

"So does that mean you're a cheer*leader*—or a cheer-*follower*?" Halley raised her brunette eyebrows.

That was *it*. Avalon glared at the girl she'd once called her best friend. A dozen kids were standing near the driveway, clearly listening to every word Halley and Avalon exchanged.

Before Avalon could go into damage-control mode, she heard a familiar horn honking. She turned and saw her *own* mother sitting in her silver BMW convertible, with Abigail Brandon in the passenger seat and Pucci in the back.

"What's *your* mom doing here?" Halley muttered as she slunk toward the car.

"I don't know," Avalon grumbled, trying to compose herself as she followed Halley.

"Hey, you two!" Constance beamed through her tortoise-shell YSL sunglasses. Her chin-length platinum hair was windblown from having the top down, but her sleeveless blue-striped Ralph Lauren oxford and beige linen capris were still perfectly crisp.

"Hi, girls." Halley's mom waved, casually tossing her long auburn hair behind her shoulders. Avalon used to think Abigail's vintage music tees (today's was David Bowie in baby pink) and teenager-at-heart hipster attitude were cool. Now she realized being a former Hollywood music exec just meant she was an immature, professional rock-wannabe.

Like mother, like daughter.

"Hi, Mom. Hi, Abby." Avalon tried to force a smile as she climbed into the car behind Constance and smothered Pucci with kisses. At least the puppy was a barrier between her and Halley. "What are you both doing here?"

"Yeah," Halley said, giving her mom a quick peck on the cheek before climbing in behind her. "What's up with that?"

"We have a big surpri-*ize*," Constance practically sang, checking her berry-red lipstick in the rearview mirror.

The last surprise The Moms had given the girls was a teeny-tiny Pucci, all snuggled up in a big blue Tiffany box for their seventh-grade graduation present.

"We've booked Nate's! We've decided to let you have your party!" Constance said, pulling out of the school gates and guiding the car down a steep, winding hill as the crystal waters washed toward the sandstone cliffs in the distance.

A shiver of excitement raced down Avalon's spine. Nate's

was one of the most popular restaurants in town. Her sister had gone to a bunch of sweet sixteens there, and she was always talking about how amazing it was—ultramodern with panoramic views of La Jolla Cove. Avalon had spent all summer dreaming about this party, and now it was finally happening!

Avalon turned excitedly to her best friend, but Halley just stared straight ahead. Make that her *ex*–best friend. How would she explain *that* one to The Moms?

"They already had something else on the calendar, but between Connie's amazing litigation skills and Dad's connections, they were willing to reshuffle things to accommodate us," Abigail continued, turning to look at the girls through her silver-rimmed aviator sunglasses.

"And more good news," Constance went on. "We're going there tonight for our family dinner, so you can design your own menus!"

Avalon didn't know whether to be stoked or sad. Nate's would be an awesome place to celebrate Halley and Avalon's friendship . . . *if* they were still friends. They couldn't exactly tell The Moms the party was probably off, and so was their friendship. Halley swiveled her head and looked directly at Avalon, her blue eyes twinkling. Halley hadn't even been excited about the party when they *were* getting along. So what had her so happy now?

For the first time in her life, Avalon didn't know how to read Halley's expression. And she couldn't think of anything scarier.

Crazy Nate's

"Is this great or what?" Charles Brandon smiled so wide, his teeth sparkled as brightly as his gray-blue eyes in the late-afternoon sun. With two-day stubble on his deeply tanned square jaw, light brown hair flopping over his forehead, and a simple white T-shirt under a black V-neck sweater, he looked like he should be sharing a beer with the laid-back surfers hanging out on the Nate's rooftop terrace.

Halley squeezed her dad's arm. "Thank you so much for getting us in here."

"And thank *you*, Mom," Avalon cooed emphatically as she adjusted her silky teal halter top.

Halley did an internal eye roll. It was so typical of Avalon to act like her family was responsible for everything even though *Halley's dad* was the one with the restaurant connections. Charles knew *the* Nate behind Nate's from producing a *Catch It, Eat It* special for the Food Network. Halley loved how hip and creative her parents were, and suddenly found herself wondering how it was possible for them to have anything in common with Avalon's parents— two lawyers.

"Right this way." A waiter with bleached hair and two turquoise studs in his ears motioned toward the other side of the patio. Halley sat between her dad and Tyler at an extra-long table overlooking the bluffs below. Fortunately, her mom and Avalon's parents made up three additional bodies separating her from Avalon and her sister, Courtney. "Love the boots, btw," the waiter said as he pulled out Halley's white-cushioned bamboo chair.

"Totally, Halley," Avalon agreed brightly, tucking herself into a chair across from Halley and sneering at Halley's black Diesel dress. "But what funeral are we going to?"

"The one where we bury the other ninety percent of your skirt." Halley nodded toward Avalon's ultrashort brown suede mini. "I guess that's what happens when you take your fashion cues from girls who have to practice spelling *lions*."

Avalon put on her biggest, fakest, cheeriest smile. The rest of their family members glanced at one another in confusion.

In spite of having to look at Avalon's plastic, peppy face across the table, Halley felt like a major A-lister as she soaked up the scene at Nate's. Everybody looked tanned and fabulous as they sipped their cocktails, the deep blue ocean gently rippling in the distance while a light breeze blew. Halley wished she'd brought her camera so she could take a picture of the amazing orange-and-lavender sky that grew richer in color as the sun slowly sank toward the Pacific. She was already imagining the sketch she'd do of it when she got home.

"Here are your first-course tasting options, everyone." Their waiter reappeared with several plates. He went through the many iterations of calamari—baked, fried, steamed, and grilled—and moved on to the oyster selection. Then came the stuffed mushroom caps, crab cakes, and roasted-beet salad. "If you have any questions, my name's Steven."

The parents all thanked Steven and began taking bites of the various appetizer options. Courtney and Tyler were locked in a debate over which was better, the grilled or fried calamari.

"S-a-l-t, could you pass the salt here, please?" Halley enunciated, taking a serving of beet salad. Avalon glared at her and shoved the salt in Halley's direction. Halley gave her a V-for-victory pose in thanks.

"Your form was a little off on that," Avalon said with fake concern. "But good effort. Maybe the squad will need some wannabes next year?"

Halley responded by noisily slurping up an oyster on the half shell, knowing exactly how gross it looked.

"Oh, grow *up*," Avalon moaned under her breath.

"Better to grow up than *out*, right?" Halley sneered back devilishly, while Avalon self-consciously wrapped her bright pink pashmina tightly around her upper body.

The Greenes and Brandons exchanged another confused look.

"What is going *on* with you two?" Abigail asked, taking a sip of her chardonnay.

"Why don't you ask *her*?" Halley replied, whipping her head toward Avalon. She couldn't wait to watch Avalon squirm through an explanation.

"Avalon?" Constance looked to her daughter for an answer as she wrapped her husband's navy-blue blazer around her shoulders. She'd already asked two waiters to turn up the heat lamps, but was still shivering in her orange chiffon tank dress.

"I don't know what to tell you." Avalon feigned innocence, pushing aside the rest of her salad.

"Come on, Avalon, tell them," Halley prompted. "Please, please, please," she fake-whined. "I'm sure everyone is *dying* to know what you have planned for our *friendship* celebration. Come on, *telllll usssss, pleeeeeeeze*."

"Jeez, I didn't know you were having *whine* with dinner," Tyler whispered.

"How is everything?" Their bleached-haired waiter appeared behind Courtney. No one answered. "Okay, then, I'll just bring the next course."

"Well, whatever this is about, it will all be forgotten by tomorrow," Abigail said as soon as Steven left.

"That's how lovers' spats usually work," Tyler smirked.

Halley shook her head and stared at her plate. There was no way she'd forget all the things Avalon had said about her clothes, about Sofee, about Wade—not to mention how controlling Avalon was, actually trying to tell her where she could hang out on campus and when she could and couldn't see her puppy!

Courtney laughed. "I don't know. I can see it on the cover of *Us Weekly*. Halvalon: *SPLIT!*"

Before Halley could respond, Steven returned with the next course and began to describe each one's ingredients in painstaking detail.

"Remember how you two used to build sand castles together, right down there on the beach?" Charles said as soon as the waiter was gone, in a useless attempt to make everything better.

"I remember how she used to *kick* sand castles in my *face*," Halley muttered.

"That's because *she* was always building them too close to the shoreline, so they got washed away before we even finished," Avalon shot back.

Charles cleared his throat. The Moms looked at each other. Avalon angrily jabbed a fork into her filet mignon. Halley took a forkful of broccolini and contemplated flinging it at Avalon's annoying blond head.

"Well, don't expect the rest of us to take sides," Abigail chimed in, looking first at Halley and then at Avalon.

"That's right," Constance agreed. "And we aren't going anywhere until you figure this out."

"Oh, so you mean we're spending the night at Nate's?" Halley smirked. Not that she would mind. The oceanside terrace was beautiful. And it might just give Halley the chance to toss Avalon overboard once and for all.

SCHOOL NEWS | HEALTH | SPORTS | ENTERTAINMENT | COMPETITION

Bust a Rut
by Style Snark B

posted: friday, 9/12, at 7:19 a.m.

Hey, kids: Time to dish about a disturbing trend I've noticed since school started. Specifically, it seems some of you are seriously scared to try something new, so you keep falling back on the same old safe, snooze-worthy styles. You may be wearing something from this season, but if you can't reinvent yourself . . . you're stuck in a rut. No, you don't need to trash your stuff altogether—you just need to make some tweaks, like so:

FASHION RUT #1: Argyle Overload. Preppy can be cute, but not if it's too buttoned-up and (yawn) *booo*-ring.

RUT-BUSTER: Mix It Up. Try throwing on a wide metallic belt, bright Bermuda shorts, or a shiny pair of sneaks, and you'll instantly go from conservative to übercool.

FASHION RUT #2: Exposed Toes. Hate to break it to those of you who can't stop showing off your pedicures, but living in SoCal doesn't need to equal flip-flops and sandals *every single day*.

RUT-BUSTER: Give 'Em the Boot. Whether it's cowboys, ankles, fold-overs, knee-highs . . . these are the shoes that can't lose, and they *always* pump up a look that's otherwise passé.

FASHION RUT #3: Skimping Out. I know there was some Snark-y advice about flaunting it if you've got it—but there's really no reason to wear last season's size with *this* season's body!

RUT-BUSTER: Cover Up. Go ahead: Try on something that actually fits rather than making yourself (and everyone around you) uncomfortable. ☺

Bottom line? Stop putting the "dud" in duds. A true fashion leader dares to be different and mixes things up when necessary.

Word to your closet,
Halley Brandon

Ha! Love what U said about skimping out. And you're right: Boots rock, and so do U. Go on with your bad self.

posted by rockgirrrl **on 9/12 at 7:30 a.m.**

Seriously? I don't think it's bad to show a little skin. I'm still on board with the "got it, flaunt it" attitude. And what's up with you and Avalon, anyway?

posted by madameprez **on 9/12 at 7:42 a.m.**

Good call on the boots! I adore your purple ones. Can I borrow? xo

posted by veepme **on 9/12 at 7:57 a.m.**

Preppy is not boring! It's classy—unlike U.

posted by brainy_blonde **on 9/12 at 8:37 a.m.**

Say cheese

"*A* little to the left . . . Wade, look right at me. . . . Give me your sexiest smile. . . . Love the lens. . . ."

Halley quietly rehearsed her most official-sounding photography directions as she walked to the music room from gymnastics practice. It had barely been twenty-four hours since she'd bailed on rehearsal, but each minute seemed like an eternity when it was spent away from Wade. Now Halley was finally going to see him again— and take pictures of him that she could gaze at whenever she wanted to.

Even though the "official" reason for this photo shoot was to get a picture to inspire her flyer sketches, a few extra shots of the lead singer couldn't hurt, right?

"Who's ready for their close-up?" Halley stood in the silver-painted doorway of the music room. She tucked a lock of wavy dark hair behind her ear. Sofee and Mason swiveled on their music-note chairs and grinned at Halley.

"The light is perfect outside right now," Halley went on, willing Wade to turn away from the sheet music he was studying. "Late-day sun is really flattering."

Wade finally turned around and stood up. In his blue Dickies work shirt and dark jeans, with his hair perfectly shaped into an even cuter fauxhawk than usual, he'd obviously made an effort to look his rock-star best. But was it all for the pictures . . . or for *Halley,* too? He fixed his eyes on hers as if she were the only person in the room. "Hot."

Did he mean hot, like good idea? Or hot, like it was the only word he could think of when he saw Halley?

Halley led the band out to the Garden of Serenity, where a small waterfall cascaded down a granite rock sculpture and beneath a Buddha statue. A weeping willow shaded a koi pond and stone bench. Halley used to come here with Avalon to drink smoothies or eat lunch. Now she was determined to create a new memory, an even better one: the day Wade fell in love with her.

"Okay, guys, let's start in front of the waterfall." She directed the band through a series of poses. There was the shot of the band huddled around Buddha. One of them goofing around on the bench beneath the weeping willow. One of them seated next to the koi pond, Sofee sprawled across their laps. And then approximately fifty of Wade. His eyes.

His lips. His elbow. She couldn't keep the zoom on her digital camera from focusing on Wade.

"So! Can we see?" Sofee reached for the camera.

"Um . . ." A bunch of close-ups of Wade wouldn't exactly impress the band with her professionalism. "I'll send you the best ones later. It's so hard to really see the pictures here anyway. Besides . . . you know I'm way better at sketching than photography. These *are* just to help me get an accurate illustration—right?"

"Totally." Wade smiled, resting his hand on the back of a bench.

Halley grinned.

"Maybe you should come take some shots at our show this weekend, just to make sure you have enough good ones?" Mason asked eagerly, tossing a pebble at a bright orange fish in the koi pond.

Wade looked down at his feet. "I don't think that's a good idea."

"Aw, come on." Sofee jabbed Wade's side. "Don't be shy."

"Yeah, that's my job," Evan said, swatting at a lock of curly hair drooping over his eyes.

Halley looked from Wade to Sofee to Evan and back. What were they talking about? The show on the flyer wasn't supposed to happen until next month.

"We're playing a super-exclusive birthday bash on Sunday," Sofee finally explained. She slid her thick, star-studded black leather bracelet up and down her slender wrist. "You should come."

A party with *Wade?* Maybe they'd even get a chance to be alone. "That sounds great," she said.

"Cool." Sofee smiled. "Hey, so Halley and I are heading out."

We are? Halley thought. *So soon?*

"Bye." Mason grabbed another pebble and chucked it in the pond. Wade and Even then joined in what appeared to be a koi-pelting contest.

"Try not to kill all the fish," Sofee added before grabbing Halley's arm.

Halley laughed and glanced back at the boys. Wade was looking directly at her. Her insides felt like a roasted marshmallow—gooey and melty and deliciously sweet.

"See you Sunday?" Wade asked.

"Yup, we'll be there," Sofee called back, grabbing her satchel.

Halley slid her camera into her messenger bag, trying to hide the grin that had spread across her face. She'd *definitely* see him Sunday. And she hoped he'd see her in a whole new light.

Snark Attack!

by Style Snark A

posted: saturday, 9/13, at 9:32 a.m.

Well, the first week of school has come and gone, and I know you're all dying for a fashion wrap-up, so here it is! A little game of YES, NO, MAYBE:

Call me catty, but I have to say that my fellow Style Snark wins the *extreme* NO award for her footwear. There were occasional moments of fashion inspiration, but only when the boots came off.

As for the MAYBE of the week, I have to give props to Margie Herring for most improved. There's absolutely nothing wrong with shopping at thrift stores (as long as you get everything professionally cleaned before wearing it, okay, *Olive?*). Next time, though, try heading for the used *women's* clothing, and you'll have a better shot of looking like Kelly Osbourne—instead of her brother! Nothing says *oops* like a pair of man-pants on a girl.

And finally . . . the YES of the week (if not the *year*) goes to (drum roll, please!): *a teacher*?! *Yes*, my friends. She's the style icon we all love to love. Go on and take a bow in those *darling* gaucho pants or your *stellar* jacquard shift, Miss Frey! (Was that Diane von Furstenberg, btw?) You are *so beyond* a YES.

That's all for now, everyone. Have a great weekend!

Shop on,
Avalon Greene

COMMENTS (201)

Yikes. The Snarks really are splitso, huh? Agree about the boot thing! Kisses . . .
posted by luv2gossip **on 9/13 at 9:51 a.m.**

Could you brown-nose a little more? LAME!
posted by justagirrrl **on 9/13 at 10:03 a.m.**

Ooooh, how scary to make your fashion wrap-up list. Like anybody cares what U think?
posted by dissect_this **on 9/13 at 10:17 a.m.**

Can u give some guy tips in ur colum bsides the man-pants thing? We need help 2.
posted by sk8punk **on 9/13 at 11:49 a.m.**

The gloves are off. . . . Maybe Mark should write about this TKO in his column!
posted by tuffprincess **on 9/13 at 11:53 a.m.**

Guess who's coming to dinner

"*B*ut we just *had* dinner with them!" Avalon groaned, tugging at the drawstring on her favorite blue cotton pajama shorts.

She was sitting with one leg tucked underneath her on a distressed oak chair in the Greenes' breakfast nook, lamenting the fact that her mother had decided to organize a late-afternoon barbecue with the Brandons. It was such an obvious ploy to force Halley and Avalon together, like some sort of kiss-and-make-up-intervention. What would be next? Couples therapy? Relationship rehab?

"Avalon, we told you the other night. You girls are welcome to argue, but it will not get in the way of us spending time with the Brandons." Constance spoke like she was addressing a hostile witness. That was how Avalon's mom always managed to get what she wanted from her daughters, her husband, and even the defendants she prosecuted—whether it was model behavior, a new diamond necklace, or twenty to life.

Annoyed as she was by the mandatory family fun, Avalon realized that if she was going to win this argument with Constance Greene, deputy district attorney—not to mention hold on to her party *sans* Halley—she needed to stop letting her mother meddle and start coming up with some ironclad excuses for bailing on the Brandons.

"The thing is, I already made cheer-practice plans with Brianna," she said, setting down her Waterford crystal tumbler of freshly squeezed orange juice next to the NUMBER ONE DAD coffee mug Avalon had made for her father when she was eight. She looked out the bay windows overlooking the backyard, past her dad and Courtney, who were reading the op-ed and style sections of the *San Diego Union-Tribune*. Martin Greene raised and lowered his bushy black eyebrows so they danced like a pair of caterpillars above his hazel eyes. "I was thinking about inviting her to spend the night."

"Well, that's fine." Constance smiled and put down the sudoku game she'd been working on to look across the table at Avalon. "Brianna can come, too. The more, the merrier."

"But how can we *practice* if we're having dinner next door?" Avalon demanded. *Especially in the presence of Halley, the ultimate persecutor of pep?* she added silently.

"You can practice *after* dinner," Constance said matter-of-factly, taking a sip of espresso from a tiny white cup.

"But . . ." Avalon leaned over and wrapped her arms around Pucci, who was sitting in the chair next to hers as if she were waiting for breakfast to be served. She rested her blond head on top of Pucci's and tried to duplicate her big, sad puppy-dog eyes.

"But *what*?" Constance shook her head at her daughter, carefully placed her cup on her empty plate, and carried the dishes over to the stainless steel sink, signaling both the end of her meal and of her conversation with Avalon.

Avalon fed her last bite of blueberry bagel to Pucci. As her mother scurried around the kitchen in her cream-colored velour sweats, wiping down the already-gleaming light wood cabinets and dark granite countertops, Avalon tried to picture the awful scene of Brianna and Halley *together* at dinner.

And then she realized: This could be fun.

That afternoon, Brianna walked through the Greenes' elegant oak front door, a giant bouquet of calla lilies in hand. Avalon gave her a tight hug that was half "I'm happy to see you" and half "Thank you for rescuing me from guaranteed family un-fun."

"So, I want to run something by you." Brianna creased her eyebrows as Avalon took the flowers from her and led her toward the kitchen.

"We're not going to be able to get you a new uniform before the first game of the season," Brianna continued apologetically. "I know this sounds crazy, but I'm pretty sure you're the same size as Amy—the squad member who moved. The only thing is that her sweater has her initials on it, but we can totally work on turning her AC into your AG! Would it give you a complete identity crisis to wear her uniform until yours arrives?"

Avalon tried not to shudder at the thought of wearing the clothes of someone she hardly knew—especially an *athletic* uniform. It sounded like a thrift-store shopping dare gone wrong.

"Of course not!" Avalon put on her peppiest voice as she placed the long-stemmed lilies in a large rectangular vase. "Anything to cheer as soon as possible!"

"Golly, you just keep proving yourself in spades." Brianna smiled.

Avalon couldn't believe someone under the age of seventy had just said *golly*, and *in spades*, but even that didn't faze her. In fact, she was so giddy over her new life as a cheerleader, she'd almost forgotten that she'd have to deal with Halley when she walked outside.

Avalon guided Brianna through the fence that separated her backyard from Halley's. The sun was setting, and the pink clouds reflected in the Greenes' gleaming infinity pool.

"Hey, everyone, this is Brianna Cho, my cheer captain,"

Avalon announced to the Brandon clan. Halley's dad was stationed at the grill, flipping organic turkey-burger patties. Tyler waved from the table.

Abigail smiled. "Nice to meet a new friend of Avalon's."

Halley didn't even try to conceal her shock.

Score one for Avalon.

"Hi, Halley. How's gymnastics going?" Brianna asked sweetly.

In her continuing quest to embrace dirty rocker chic, Halley was wearing some lame-looking Mom-me-down concert tee that said CROWDED HOUSE: DON'T DREAM IT'S OVER and wrinkled cut-off jean shorts. Ick.

"Strongest team we've ever had, now that we cut the fat," she replied, staring at Avalon's chest.

The girls sat down at a patio table. Constance and Courtney headed inside to help Abigail with the salads and side dishes. Tyler headed over to the barbecue, where Martin had joined Charles.

Just as Avalon was creating a mental chart with all the pros of being friends with Brianna (starting with her adorable red tank, khaki cargoes, and gold patent ballet flats) and cons of being friends with Halley (starting with today's ensemble), Halley asked the unthinkable:

"How's the squad this year, Brianna?"

"It's great, thanks so much for—"

"We'll show you how great it is," Avalon interrupted.

Finally, she had her chance to show her ex-bestie how her Halley-free life was treating her.

Halley's face clouded over. Avalon grabbed Brianna's hand and led her over to the big grassy area in front of Halley's old stone playhouse for a killer version of "We're Awesome."

"Ready? Okay!" Brianna led off. The girls proceeded through the whole cheer, hitting every note and even finishing it off with an impromptu back-handspring at the end.

The parents had gathered to watch, and they whooped at the performance. Tyler gave them two enthusiastic thumbs-up. Courtney even smiled and nodded her approval from the deck.

Avalon looked over at Halley, just in time to see her fake-barfing over the side of her chair. That was all she needed. She'd officially made Halley sick, and she didn't care if it was with jealousy or disgust. Score one for Avalon.

Prêt-à-Partay
by Style Snark B

posted: sunday, 9/14, at 9:57 a.m.

Hey, kids: If it's the weekend, then you *know* it's time to let go of the past and *party*! Of course, the biggest dilemma on every socialite's calendar is *what to wear* to all those stellar soirees. Well, I'm here to tell you that you've basically got two options: You can either go all-out, over-the-top, catwalk crazy, and work it like a madwoman, meaning knee-high boots, leather and suede, patterns and prints—nothing's shocking! *Or*, you can bust out the classic with a twist—neutral colors (blacks, whites, and beiges) and simple fabrics (denim, cotton, and linen), then throw 'em a curveball with rhinestone embellishments, sparkly shoes, or brightly colored accessories so you don't blend into the background (remember, *boooring* is *baaad*). Go with either extreme and, voilà! You're the belle of the ball. . . .

Word to your closet,

Halley Brandon

Bring back Snark A! This advice is so boring, it put me to sleep. Zzzzz.

posted by hotterthanU **on 9/14 at 10:32 a.m.**

Whatever 2 "hotterthanU." Maybe you just have snarkolepsy! ☺ I like Snark B way better than Snark A and this is awesome advice. Thx.

posted by rockgirrrl **on 9/14 at 11:21 a.m.**

Kute kolum. I opt for katwalk kraaaazy! Party on, Snark B.

posted by kre8ivekween **on 9/14 at 11:59 a.m.**

Snark A is sassier but Snark B is smarter. I like 'em both!

posted by madameprez **on 9/14 at 12:30 p.m.**

Wade's world

 alley was completely speechless. There she was, in *Wade Houston's* backyard, with the guy she'd been fantasizing about all week singing his heart out under a big white party tent. She had tortured herself over what to wear. In the end, she'd opted for a funky-casual look— gray denim miniskirt, big white belt, and a black bedazzled tank with glittery silver wedges—which turned out to be the perfect ensemble for this, the super-exclusive birthday party of . . .

Wade's four-year-old brother, Johnny.

It seemed like every child under the age of five in the county had been invited to celebrate the littlest Houston. His family made friends fast. Johnny had a square, feature-less face, made even squarer by his dirty-blond crew cut and buckteeth. Halley thought SpongeBob would have been an ideal theme for the party, given poor Johnny's appearance, and she wondered if he and Wade were really related. Wade didn't resemble his parents either, who were pictures of San Francisco hippiedom with their long stringy hair, little round glasses, and bohemian peasant clothes.

"You're pwetty!" squeaked a voice from somewhere around Halley's waist.

Halley looked down to see a round, freckle-covered boy with fiery red hair and a striped green polo shirt.

"Aw, thank you." Halley smiled at her miniature fan. "And you're very handsome."

Halley tried not to laugh at the little guy, who reminded her of one of the Myerson triplets she and Avalon used to babysit (although she could never tell the three boys—Mark, Matan, and Morris—apart). For a second, she wanted to call Avalon and tell her all about where she was and what she was doing, but quickly realized with a pang that Avalon was completely uninterested in the Dead Romeos—and in Halley, for that matter.

"What's your name?" Halley asked in the singsong voice she reserved for toddlers.

"Donovan!" the boy declared. "Wanna dance wiv me?"

"Of course!" Halley said as Donovan dragged her toward the tent, where the Dead Romeos were in the middle of their set.

The entire band was dressed just like the Wiggles, in

matching black pants and brightly colored long-sleeved shirts. Wade was the yellow Wiggle, Sofee was red, Evan was purple, and Mason was blue. Someone was wearing a Wags the Dog costume, bouncing around the group as they all sang "Toot Toot, Chugga Chugga, Big Red Car."

Halley happily swung Donovan around in circles. After all, she'd probably be spending lots of time with all of Johnny's friends when she and Wade became an official couple. When she was finally sweaty and out of breath, Halley told Donovan she needed to go get a drink.

"They have Clifford juice over there!" Donovan squealed, pointing to three long, yellow, crepe paper–covered tables on the opposite side of the yard.

"Cool." Halley smiled and eased through a maze of kids, toy cars, beach balls, and boat-shaped sandboxes. Among the lavish spread of treats designed for the preschool set were several bowls full of juice boxes.

Halley pulled a Clifford apple juice from the icy bowl, grabbed a handful of eggshell-blue M&M's, and headed over to a miniature plastic red table to watch the rest of the Wiggles set. And by that, she meant scrutinize every visible detail of Wade's home.

Halley could picture Wade reading *Rolling Stone* in the old blue net hammock that was tied between two oak trees. She imagined him lightly strumming an acoustic guitar on the back porch of the gray bungalow-style house. She saw him walking the three blocks to the beach. She imagined that before long, he'd be picking the yellow roses from the back fence and offering them to Halley.

"Hey." Sofee came skipping over. Halley snapped to attention. She hadn't even noticed that the music had switched to a Backyardigans CD. Even dressed as a Wiggle, with her black curls tied into two Princess Leia–style buns on either side of her head, Sofee looked phenomenal. "Can you believe this?"

"It's hilarious." Halley grinned, popping a few final M&M's into her mouth and standing. "Wade's little brother is adorable."

"So, how's the Clifford juice?" Sofee asked, grinning at the little green box in Halley's hand. "I hear apple is their specialty."

"Oh, it's delicious, and *so* refreshing," Halley deadpanned.

"We're gonna pack up our things and get out of here pretty soon," Sofee told Halley. "Wanna help?"

"Sure," Halley offered, following Sofee over to the tent, where Wade and the boys were putting away their equipment.

"Hey, did you get some good shots?" Mason smirked at Halley. "I really think blue is my color."

"Yeah." Halley smiled. "I'm pretty impressed you guys even allowed me to bring a camera in here."

"We have no shame!" Mason yelled, pretending to hit a set of imaginary drums, his blond hair whipping around wildly.

Evan smiled and rolled his eyes nervously in Halley's general direction and then squatted down to put his bass in a black Fender case.

"Can you grab one of those amps for me?" Sofee asked Halley.

"Sure." Halley walked over and picked up a small black-and-silver amp, wrapped up the cord that was plugged into it, and began carrying it toward Wade, who was looking directly at her with those dark, mesmerizing eyes. It didn't even faze Halley that Wade was dressed like a Wiggle; he was the most beautiful person she'd ever seen, and the fact that he'd embarrass himself for his little brother made him that much more amazing.

As Halley approached Wade, the amp cord unraveled and Halley stumbled, dropping the amp on the concrete path with a crash.

"Ohmygod, sorry!" Halley looked down at the amp, partly to make sure she hadn't damaged it, and partly so Wade wouldn't see the tears that were starting to sting her eyes. How could she have been so tragic?

"Don't worry about it," Wade said, gently laying his hand on Halley's bare shoulder and giving her a half smile. "No harm done. But maybe you and Sofee should just go hang inside or something."

The pressure of Wade's palm left Halley's skin feeling warmer than a new sunburn.

"Yeah, um, let's go." Sofee motioned for Halley to follow her past Arthur the Aardvark, who was sitting alone just outside the party tent.

Halley cringed, feeling like she had more in common with the bespectacled cartoon character than she'd like to admit. She plodded alongside Sofee toward the back steps of the Houstons' house, suddenly wondering what she was doing here with all these people she barely knew.

Sofee was awesome, and Wade was, obviously, the definition of perfect, but who could Halley tell her humiliating stories to when the humiliating stories involved *them*? Where was the person who would know all the right things to say? Even on their worst days, nobody understood Halley like Avalon had. And without Avalon, who did Halley *really* have left?

| SCHOOL NEWS | HEALTH | SPORTS | ENTERTAINMENT | COMPETITION |

No More *Weekend* Wear
by Style Snark A

posted: monday, 9/15, at 7:11 a.m.

If the past couple days are any indicator, some people view the weekend as an opportunity not only to dress down, but down and *out*. Well I'm here to say you can still be casual and comfortable without looking like a Pacific Beach panhandler. The fact is, trendsetters never take a day off, and you should *always* strive to look your best—especially since you never know when you might run into someone you want to impress. To make sure your Saturdays and Sundays sizzle from now on, just think P-R-A-D-A:

Primp. If you think personal hygiene is optional on the weekends, think again. Take a shower, brush your hair, and for goodness' sake, get a mani-pedi.

Reflect. Really ponder what you're wearing, and scrutinize every detail in the mirror—otherwise you'll look like a graduate of the Helen Keller School of Style.

Accessorize. It doesn't get any easier than this: Throw on a bracelet or necklace and at least *pretend* you tried.

Dominate. Don't worry about overdressing. It's way better to outshine than to be outshone.

Alternate. Recycling is for bottles and cans. Don't make us look at your ratty old T-shirt and cutoffs more than once (which was already one time too many!).

Simple enough? It should be! Have a great week, everyone. *Please.*

Shop on,
Avalon Greene

Ohmygod, thank u for saying this. I'm so tired of seeing people looking homeless just cuz it's Saturday—or cuz they're too lazy during the week, too.

posted by yazmeenie **on 9/15 at 7:17 a.m.**

You are so bad. In a good way, natch. LOVING Snark A! ☺

posted by veepme **on 9/15 at 7:31 a.m.**

U said it, sister. Snarkalicious! No more smelly weekend scumbags!

posted by superstyleme **on 9/15 at 7:47 a.m.**

What about after practice? Some of us actually work out on the weekends. Vote 4 Mark!

posted by tuffprincess **on 9/15 at 7:58 a.m.**

Cheer pressure

"Try it again," Sydney barked at the cheerleaders, her beady little violet eyes fixed on Avalon. She reminded Avalon of a celebutante's dog with her yappy voice and blond pigtails bouncing furiously on the sides of her head. She was, Avalon decided, a cheerhuahua.

Halley would have loved that one. Too bad she'd never get to hear about it.

Avalon tried to maintain her composure while glancing around at the others. "Um, exactly *what* are we doing wrong?" Avalon asked Sydney on behalf of the squad.

Brianna had missed school today and was AWOL from practice. Sydney was clearly power-tripping on her absence.

"Everything!" Sydney hopped off the bleachers and walked the squad through the new routine that *Avalon* had created with Brianna on Saturday night. This time, Sydney actually changed some of the moves. She made her grating little voice as husky as possible as she shouted the words:

Watch your front and watch your back,
We're lions and we will attack!
Awesome, rad, and super-cool,
It's true, we'll make you look like fools!
Lions, L-I-O-N-S,
Lions, lions, we're the best!
Roar, roar, roar, roar!
Yep, you betcha, we just scored!
Roar, roar, roar, roar,
Ohmygod, you still want more?
Roar, roar, roar, roar,
So long, losers, there's the door!

Avalon was at a loss. Sydney wasn't improving the cheer at all, unless you counted her circus-sideshow-like ability to make her limbs so rigid that they might actually snap. Besides, the new moves in her version were like wearing boots with shorts: awkward and just *wrong*.

Avalon walked over to the bleachers to grab her second Red Bull since lunch. Even though her stomach was beginning to burn, she realized she would need all the help she could get to stay peppy with the cheerhuahua tormenting her at every turn. Just as Avalon was setting the can down, Brianna finally arrived.

"Ohmygosh, you guys, I'm so sorry I'm late," Brianna said, her face pink and blotchy. She wore a short red Adidas sports tank and gray leggings. "So, where are we?"

Before anybody could say anything, Sydney marched over to Brianna and pulled her aside, leaving Avalon to enjoy some quick gossip with the rest of the squad. Tanya immediately low-fived Avalon for taking on Sydney.

"We're *so* over her," Andi stage-whispered to Avalon just as Brianna and Sydney broke apart. Avalon tried to discreetly wipe the spray that had hit her cheek when Andi spoke.

"Okay, everyone," Brianna yelled. She was smiling, but something was off. "Let's run through 'Watch Your Front' and really give it your all!"

The co-captains watched as the squad did the cheer for about the fifteenth time that afternoon. Sydney looked as irritated as ever, her arms crossed tightly in front of her tiny chest, but Brianna moved her body along with the girls in half-cheer poses and nodded enthusiastically, starting to look more like her usual self.

"That was awesome, you guys!" Brianna announced when they were done. "Now let's try it again, but this time let's change up the moves like this."

Brianna proceeded to modify the cheer in the same way Sydney had, adding in a kick ball change and few other random dance steps, along with a herkie at the end. Avalon couldn't believe Brianna was taking direction from Sydney on what was practically *Avalon*'s cheer.

"You know, we've been practicing the cheer since three-thirty, and I really think everyone's doing an *incredible* job with it," Avalon interjected. "Shouldn't we just stick with the moves the way they were?"

Sydney tossed her head indignantly in Brianna's direction, as if to say, "How *dare* she question *us*?"

Brianna just grinned happily and said in a firm, controlled voice, "Let's just try it this way and see how it goes."

Avalon's eyes widened, but she shut her mouth and did as she was told. She nailed the revised moves, shooting a satisfied "Take that" look in Sydney's direction at the end.

"Okay, great job!" Brianna said when practice was finally over. "Thanks for working so hard and thanks to Sydney for taking charge until I got here."

Avalon didn't want the practice to end with props for the cheerhuahua, so she decided it was the perfect time to make her party announcement.

"Hey, everybody," Avalon called after the squad as most of the girls began walking toward the bleachers. "Before you go, I just wanted to tell you all to check your e-mail. I sent you Evites to an *amazing* party, and I hope you can make it!"

Several of the girls smiled back at Avalon, but Sydney shot Brianna a look.

"Hey, you," Brianna said.

"What's up?" Avalon asked as she and Brianna strode past the bleachers and away from the football field. In the distance, the Pacific Ocean went on forever.

"Well, this is totally *not* your fault," Brianna said kindly. "But the thing is, there are certain rules I haven't told you about—not official rules, but sort of our own cheerleading code of conduct."

"Uh-huh?" Avalon nervously crunched her empty Red Bull can between her thumb and index finger.

"Well, *this* is the first thing," Brianna said, gently extracting the can from Avalon's hand and holding it up in front of her eyes. "I've noticed you drinking *a lot* of energy drinks. *Major* no-no."

Avalon couldn't believe Brianna had just said *no-no*.

"We really frown upon *any* type of artificial pep," Brianna said. Her dark eyes looked soft and wise, like she'd given this speech a million times. "Cheering is all about putting out your *natural* best."

"I just wanted to make sure I was giving it my all," Avalon explained as they continued to walk along the brick footpath toward the main SMS building.

"And that's great!" Brianna gushed. "But again, a no-no . . . and that goes for parties, too. I can't have my girls going out the night before big games, or we *obviously* won't be performing at our peak."

119

"But my party is on a Saturday—so that's okay, right?" Avalon couldn't believe she was asking for Brianna's *permission*.

"It's probably fine," Brianna said in a terse-but-still-friendly voice. "I just don't want anybody to have so much fun that they're too tired to cheer."

"Ohhh." Avalon felt like a deflating beach ball.

"So!" Brianna smiled as they finally made their way into the girls' locker room. "Are we all good?"

"Uh-huh." Avalon nodded quietly.

"Awesome!" Brianna enthused, walking along the wooden bench between two rows of blue and gold lockers.

"Awesome," Avalon replied, her voice hollow. Because she didn't feel awesome at all.

| SCHOOL NEWS | HEALTH | SPORTS | ENTERTAINMENT | **COMPETITION** |

Tears of a Clone
by Style Snark B

posted: tuesday, 9/16, at 7:11 a.m.

Clothing yourself can be *so* complicated. Of course, you want to be current and hip to what's hot—but when you work the latest trends *too* hard, you wind up looking like the Queen of Conformity. (I swear if I see one more tailored miniskirt and tight sweater, I'm going to start issuing DUIs for dressing under the influence!) That's why you need to follow these four simple rules for making a fully funkified—and forever fabulous—fashion statement:

1. **Rip it off.** See a trend you like and, basically, copy it. (Don't worry. This is just step one.)
2. **Change it up.** Once you've got the trend nailed, take something out—like the shoes or the belt—and substitute something slightly different. Now you're on your way to distinguishing yourself.

3. **Relocate.** Try putting one of the things you're wearing in a new place; for instance, how about using one of those cute dangly earrings as a brooch or maybe wearing your necklace or scarf as a belt? Wow . . . you are *so* developing your own look now, but still trendy-to-an-extreme.

4. **DIY.** Now for the pièce de résistance: Add something daring and/or completely of your own design, whether it's a homemade bracelet or a rare accessory from a thrift store (or even Mommy's closet).

Got it? Good. Now let's everybody get funked up!

Word to your closet,
Halley Brandon

Ha! Dressing under the influence. You deserve a snarking ticket. ☺

posted by rockgirrrl **on 9/16 at 7:21 a.m.**

An earring as a brooch? Do people under the age of seventy really wear brooches? And a homemade bracelet or thrift store accessory? Yikes. Somebody call 911. This fashion advice is CRIMINAL.

posted by brainy_blonde **on 9/16 at 7:43 a.m.**

Or U could spend less time getting dressed and actually go *do* something. Vote 4 David's Playlist!

posted by jimisghost **on 9/16 at 7:56 a.m.**

Funk yeah! AWESOME column, B. Word to your mother (or at least to her brooch).

posted by madameprez **on 9/16 at 8:02 a.m.**

Hugs and disses

*H*alley sat at her iMac in the journalism villa and silently congratulated herself on the column she'd written before school, which had already generated a ton of fan e-mail and only a few negative responses—one of which she was 99 percent certain had been written by Avalon. Halley had decided to take refuge in the classroom during lunch to read the latest comments because, as much as she hated to admit it, navigating the SMS dining quad had been challenging, to say the least, since she and Avalon had stopped eating together. She had tried hanging out with a few of the girls from gymnastics, but she was actually kind of disturbed when she witnessed Piggleigh Swinetraub showing three sixth-graders how to chew their food more energetically so they could burn an extra twelve calories an hour.

Halley was tired of all the questions about whether

124

she and Avalon were really over—and if so, *why*—not to mention listening to the artificial laughter that seemed to permeate every hallway of SMS whenever Avalon and her new identically dressed cheer-friends were together. Halley had really been hoping she could do lunch with Sofee and maybe even Wade. Alas, the Dead Romeos usually spent the period practicing in the music room, and Halley didn't want to follow them like a desperate groupie. Besides, even after the slightly embarrassing amp-dropping incident on Sunday, she was half-expecting Wade to come looking for *her*.

Halley continued to scroll through the comments on her column, but wasn't paying much attention to them anymore. Instead, she was listening to Snow Patrol's "Chasing Cars" on her iPod while imagining various scenarios in which Wade finally declared his love for her. Just as Halley was lost in a cozy moment in front of the fire with Wade, a streak of sunlight nearly blinded her. The door of the journalism villa opened, and Halley looked over to see Avalon walking in.

"Well, if it isn't Style Snark A," Halley said, pulling the earbuds out of her ears and setting them on the desk. She forced a confident front, silently telling herself that Avalon had become nothing more than a pathetic pep squad fashion follower in her tan wool miniskirt and short-sleeved red cardigan.

Avalon didn't say anything. She just sat down two desks

over from Halley and looked up with those soft, brown puppy-dog eyes that were oddly similar to Pucci's. With the mouse in one hand, Avalon fixed her gaze on the iMac screen in front of her and began tugging at a lock of her flaxen hair— the telltale sign that something was bothering her. It *almost* made Halley want to be nice. Almost.

"What are you doing here?" Halley asked condescendingly, staring at her own computer screen.

"I wanted to get a jump start on my column for tomorrow," Avalon replied in the softest-sounding voice Halley had ever heard come out of her mouth.

"Oh, *awesome*," Halley squealed in her best cheerleader voice. "Will it be another commentary on my inability to dress up for a backyard barbecue?"

Avalon inhaled deeply and stood up. She walked toward the front of the villa and looked at the *Daily* production schedule taped to the blackboard. "That *was* about me, wasn't it?" Halley pushed. "You know, 'don't make us look at your ratty old T-shirt more than once' or whatever?"

Avalon sighed, turning around to face Halley but still standing at the front of the room, behind Miss Frey's dark oak desk. "Kind of like today's was about what a clone I am?"

"Observant," Halley said, raising her eyebrows and cocking her head to one side as Avalon continued to tug at her hair distractedly.

Avalon looked even more exhausted than she had after

she and Halley had pulled an all-night study session last year. Today, though, Avalon's face betrayed more than just exhaustion.

"Honestly?" Avalon said flatly. "I'm having a bad week, and I don't really want to get into it with you."

Halley felt a sudden wave of pity for Avalon. She ran a fuchsia fingernail along her dark-brown cords and slid her gunmetal-silver ankle-boots back on her feet. She couldn't decide how to react.

"So you don't want to talk about it?" Halley finally offered, hoping to extract enough information to decide whether or not to empathize.

"With *you*?" Avalon asked. She hesitantly walked back toward Halley and sat down at the desk next to her. "Why would I?"

"Um, because I used to be pretty good at listening and helping you figure things out," Halley said, genuinely thinking it might be time to give Avalon the benefit of the doubt. She met Avalon's quizzical gaze.

Avalon paused for what felt like an hour, then finally spoke. "I'm just not sure about the whole cheerleading thing. I mean, they have all these rules that I think I've already broken. And . . . Brianna's awesome—*obviously*—but the rest of them have been together for so long, and one of them is kind of mean, and . . . it's just kind of hard to break into a group that tight, you know?"

"You mean that *up*tight?" Halley laughed. "Seriously, who can pretend to be that *up*beat all the time?" she joked.

But Avalon didn't seem to find it funny.

"I'm not the one pretending around here," she snapped. "What do you call running around like some poseur artiste or lovesick groupie in those stupid T-shirts and No-beyond-belief boots?"

"For the last time, I'm *not a groupie*, I'm their *publicist*!" Halley fumed, not even acknowledging the boot comment, which was getting *seriously* tired.

"Uh-huh." Avalon sneered as she jumped up from her chair and stormed toward the door. "Speaking of publicity, I was going to put you on my Evite guest list so you could see how *awesome* the Greene Party's going to be—but not anymore."

"*The Greene Party?* Like I even need an invitation to *your* party when it's *my* party, too?" Halley laughed, shaking her head incredulously.

"Um, if it's 'your party, too,' you have a funny way of showing it," Avalon snapped. "I mean, I spent the whole summer coming up with the theme, the guest list, the design concept—and The Moms and I have been the only ones organizing any of the details, with absolutely no input from you."

"I have an idea for the band," Halley said flatly. She'd been thinking about it since Wade's little brother's party. If the way to Wade's heart was through the band, then she knew how to make herself impossible for him to resist. Forget the Greene Party—it was time for Halleypalooza!

"Well, if you knew *anything* about what's been planned so far, you'd realize how redundant and unnecessary that is," Avalon shot back. "Hello? Didn't your mom even tell you she already hired DJ AM, like, a week ago?"

"*Yes,*" Halley sneered, her confidence beginning to blossom as she prepared to share a brand-new piece of party-planning info. "And when I mentioned a band to her, we decided live music *and* a DJ would be awesome."

"Oh." Avalon looked like someone had just told her Target is the new Nordstrom.

"The bigger question?" Halley continued, certain Avalon would buckle at the thought of losing her precious party without Halley's complete cooperation. "Have you told The Moms that you've changed the theme from Friendapalooza to the Greene Party?"

"Not exactly . . ." Avalon smirked, her dark eyes gleaming under the overhead lights. "I just told them to make the primary focus *fashion* instead of *friendship*."

"And you really think that's gonna fly?"

"Um, *yeah*," Avalon retorted. "Because if they question it at all . . . I know you'll back me up."

"How do you figure?" Halley demanded. She couldn't believe Avalon was assuming Halley would back her up on *anything* at this point.

"Well"—Avalon raised her pale blond eyebrows—"I know you want the party as badly as I do so the stupid Dead Shakespeares can play."

"Dead *Romeos*," Halley muttered.

"Whatever," Avalon spat. "The fact is, we need each other now. *However*, I would be *mortified* if you dragged down *my* party with your pose-a-be friends and those *talentless* wannabe rockers. So, we'll just split the party down the middle. You can take the upstairs area of Nate's, I'll take the downstairs—and we'll see who *really* rocks."

"Sounds good to me," Halley said, annoyed that Avalon just assumed she got to make all the decisions—but more than happy to party with the Dead Romeos in the absence of Avalon and all *her* lame friends. It was actually a pretty inspired solution to the whole party dilemma. "Just don't come crying to me when the cheerleaders bail on you, all the boys are up on *my* rooftop patio, and you're trying to crash Halleypalooza to find out what happens at a *real* party."

"Fine!"

"Fine!"

As the door to the villa slammed behind Avalon, Halley couldn't have been happier to rid herself of Drama Queen Greene once and for all.

Clothes That Don't Rock
by Style Snark A

posted: wednesday, 9/17, at 7:12 a.m.

We all have our favorite songs, bands, music—whatever. And that's great. Until, that is, you start taking your style cues from *TRL*. I mean, hello? You're *not* Avril freaking Lavigne, so enough with trying to look like you are. Stop putting holes in your face, wash off those fake tattoos, and nix the clunky goth boots in eighty-degree weather. You look more like *The Biggest Loser* than an *American Idol*. And P.S.: iPods are *not* fashion accessories. If you took out the earbuds, maybe you'd hear everybody dissing your delusional attempt at dressing yourself. I don't even need to name names. You NO who you are.

Shop on,
Avalon Greene

OMG! Someone's on fire today. I guess the "A" in Snark A stands for angry. Or attitude. Or Avalon is absofrigginlutely brilliant. U have my vote.

posted by veepme **on 9/17 at 7:51 a.m.**

Uh, people have been taking their fashion cues from their fave artists for YEARS. Punk, mod, glam, emo . . . any of those ring a bell? How about Gwen Stefani and L.A.M.B.? Rockstars R style icons. U R not.

posted by justagirrrl **on 9/17 at 8:03 a.m.**

justagirrl is right. Down with Halvalon.

posted by jimisghost **on 9/17 at 8:09 a.m.**

So what fashions do rock, if you're so smart? Boycott Snark A . . . Snark B is the one who knows clothes.

posted by kre8ivekween **on 9/17 at 8:17 a.m.**

LOL! If there was any question about Halvalon splitting up . . . this clears up THAT confusion. Whoa. Killer advice though. So tired of the poser look.

posted by luv2gossip **on 9/17 at 9:49 a.m.**

Pep talk

"*A*wesome job, you guys!" Brianna looked even happier than usual as she straightened the hem of her orange Adidas by Stella McCartney top. All the cheerleaders were flushed and sweaty from working on their routine in the humid seventy-five-degree heat, but Brianna was too amped to stop now. "Let's just run through 'Watch Your Front' one more time!"

Brianna beamed at Avalon as if channeling a secret message to her. They hadn't really had any one-on-one conversations since Brianna gave Avalon the rundown on her cheerleading rules two days ago, and Avalon had tried to be particularly cautious about doing anything that might violate the pep squad code of conduct.

Avalon couldn't believe she'd admitted her cheer fears to Halley—as if *she'd* understand *anything* about rules, especially new alterna-Halley. Weren't most music-obsessed creative types all about *breaking* the rules? Halley's attitude just made Avalon all the more determined to stay on track with the pep squad, so she'd decided to speak only when spoken to, avoid gossiping—even about Sydney—and focus on being the most energetic cheerleader she could be.

"Let's finish up with the Crazy V!" Brianna shouted as they wrapped up the cheer. As Avalon moved into formation with the others and yelled, "Get rowdy, get rough, Lions strut your stuff," she decided this was her chance to show the girls that she was still the same person they'd been so excited to vote onto the squad last week. She followed along with the dance moves and waited for her turn to tumble. When she was finally up, she showcased a roundoff, back handsprings/ back tuck/splits combo she was sure would blow them all away. It worked. All the girls went wild. Even Sydney looked impressed.

"That was so awesome!" squealed Gabrielle Velasquez, the twin sister of Anna from journalism class. Gabby and Anna were both voluptuous but Gabby had longer, darker curls and was always suited up in Lycra tanks and leggings. Avalon was actually waiting for the right moment to find out where she got her tops, since they seemed to do a great job at keeping her extreme curves under control.

"Seriously, your back-handsprings are incredible!" Andi Lynch agreed, spittle spraying from her pink lips when she said *spring*. The tiny freckled brunette was wearing black capris and a formfitting red tank. By now, Avalon knew to turn her head away when Andi spoke.

"Thanks." Avalon smiled. "I guess all those years of gymnastics are paying off."

"They sure are," Brianna enthused. "Do you guys mind if I steal Avalon for a minute?"

"Of course not!" Andi shouted. Avalon noticed Gabby wiping moisture from her upper arm and moving a little farther away from Andi as they walked off with the rest of the squad.

"Long time, no chat." Avalon smiled as she and Brianna slowly headed away from the football field. She tried to stay upbeat, but was half-wondering if Brianna thought she had been showing off on her last tumbling pass.

Maybe there are rules about out-cheering each other, Avalon thought only half-sarcastically.

"So," Brianna began, running her hand over her shiny black ponytail. "I wanted to say I'm sorry if I was too hard on you the other day."

Avalon wiped her sweaty palms on her heather-gray Roxy sweatshorts and gave Brianna a grateful smile.

"I just don't want the others to think I'm giving you preferential treatment, you know?" Brianna continued. "But I think you're doing such an amazing job, and we're all so happy to have you on the squad."

"And I'm really happy to *be* on the squad," Avalon replied, meaning every word as she exhaled deeply.

"Oh, good," Brianna said. "I also wanted to tell you I'm having a squad sleepover after the game this Friday. Can you come?"

Avalon felt the same rush of acceptance she'd experienced when she'd made the squad, like everything was finally falling into place again. She was about to accept Brianna's invitation, but then remembered *CosmoGIRL!*'s advice on fitting in with new friends. *Be inviting: Getting to know people on your home turf puts you in a power-position and makes you more comfy and confident.*

"Totally," Avalon said. "Unless, maybe, is there any chance you'd let *me* host the sleepover?"

As they neared the main SMS building, Brianna gave Avalon a tell-me-more look.

"It's just that I really want everyone to see how excited I am about being on the squad," Avalon explained, searching Brianna's face for a reaction. "You know, they just don't know me as well as you do, and seeing me in my own environment would probably help. Don't you think?"

"*Great* idea." Brianna nodded as they arrived in the school lobby and turned to head toward the girls' locker room. "I'll send out an e-mail announcement tonight!"

Avalon was beyond stoked. It wouldn't just be a slumber party—it would be the slumber party to end all slumber parties. She would *definitely* win over the squad, and then her new life as a cheerleader would be complete. Talk about trading up: She'd ditched one smelly old poseur friend for nine amazing new ones!

Take Out the Trash

by Style Snark B

posted: thursday, 9/18, at 7:16 a.m.

We live in a city where the sun rarely stops shining, and that's usually a good thing—until, of course, the sweltering temperatures become an excuse for extreme overexposure. Seriously, if people are having a tough time figuring out if you meant to forget your pants, you're showing too much skin. (You honestly expect us to believe that's a dress? Thanks for playing. Please try again.)

Not to be a prude, but come on. Weren't you paying attention when we said that one of the Four C's of style is Class? Step away from that micromini! Nobody should expose that much leg (or booty). And enough with the low-cut halter tops. Stop wearing your desperation on your sleeve, your sweater, your skirt—wherever—and cover up a little bit!

Word to your closet,

Halley Brandon

Awesomely said. I'm so tired of the skankatrons in this school.

posted by sassmasterflash **on 9/18 at 7:27 a.m.**

Good call. And can we add tube-tops to the please-don't-go-there list? They're a wardrobe malfunction waiting 2 happen, especially on the more boobalicious of us.

posted by madameprez **on 9/18 at 7:43 a.m.**

Can you give us an appropriate dress-length to shoot for? Should it be just below the butt or like mid-thigh, or what?

posted by miss_fit **on 9/18 at 8:18 a.m.**

Here's a hint, miss_fit: If you have to ask, it's too short!

posted by tuffprincess **on 9/18 at 8:23 a.m.**

Power plays

"You're totally going down—*again!*" Halley screamed as she jumped up and down on her brother's crumpled silver comforter, taunting him with the PlayStation controller. They'd been locked in an epic Tekken battle since Halley had gotten home from gymnastics, and things had become so competitive that Tyler had actually tossed a not-quite-empty cup of Dr Pepper at Halley's head, drenching her hair and leotard with dark, sticky liquid. But she was having too much fun to be annoyed—or give up. She just threw on one of her brother's dry, albeit stained, *Star Wars* shirts and kept on playing.

In stark contrast to the bright, open, airy feel of the rest of the Brandon house, Tyler's room was like a dungeon. It was just off the garage, and although it was a decent-size space, the only light sources were two small windows and an old stainless steel ceiling fan with one working bulb. The bluish-black walls plastered with *Star Wars* and *Lord of the Rings* posters didn't help. Tyler hadn't redecorated since he was ten, despite their parents' annual offer to bring in professional help, and it smelled like a few of the half-eaten specimens on his beat-up oak desk dated back at least that far. The only new and well-maintained possessions in the room were his iMac, PlayStation, and plasma HDTV.

"You don't have to play anymore if you don't want to," Tyler said, which sounded more like a plea for mercy than like an offer to let her off the hook.

"That's okay." Halley grinned as she leapt off the mock-spaceship bed onto the gray Berber carpet to sit next to Pucci and began scratching behind her puppy ears. "I've got a few minutes before Sofee gets here."

Halley knew it was slightly pathetic that Tyler had become her primary source of entertainment in the past week. But even if Sofee hadn't been completely booked with Dead Romeos rehearsals, hanging with Tyler was kind of a nice break from the drama of Halley's post-Avalon world. Besides, Tyler's room had become the coolest part of the house—in temperature only, of course—since her parents had decided it was time to conserve energy and stop using the AC now that it was fall. Because Tyler's room was the only bedroom on the first floor and there was some good cross-ventilation coming through the open garage door, they were *almost* managing to keep themselves from sweating to death.

"Fine, but at least show me how to do that twirl and ground kick you used last time." Tyler pushed a dark wave of hair out of his blue eyes and sat down on the other side of Pucci.

"Oh, I'll show you," Halley said. "Right . . . *now!*" She hit a series of buttons on her controller and proceeded to make her character knock Tyler's out instantly, then jumped up and did a high-knee-bending lap around the room, making fake breathy-applause noises with her throat and shouting, "Asuka Kazama cannot be stopped! Prepare for the next battle!" as she pumped her arms in the air.

"Um, Hal?" Tyler said nonchalantly, rubbing Pucci's belly and raising one eyebrow at his sister.

"What?"

"Company," Tyler replied with a smirk, moving only his eyes toward the bedroom door. Pucci barked and jumped up, running to slobber all over . . .

Wade.

"Pucci, down!" Halley said, darting toward the puppy. "Ohmygod, I'm so sorry!" She knelt down and tugged on Pucci's yellow-and-blue scarf. Of course, she wasn't exactly sure what she was sorriest for—the slobber Pucci had dribbled all over Wade's dark jeans and Docs, the smell of her brother's room, or the fact that she had just made the most geeked-out spectacle of herself in the history of geeked-out spectacles, while covered in soda and wearing a WHO'S YOUR JEDI? shirt. This made the amp-dropping incident look like a flawlessly choreographed gymnastics performance.

"No problem." Wade laughed and crouched down next to Halley, fixing his dark eyes on hers. "Your mom let me in. Sorry I didn't call first—I didn't have your number, so I thought I'd just stop by, and—"

"That's okay," Halley interrupted. She couldn't believe how nervous he seemed!

Tyler grinned and got up from the floor. "I'm Tyler. The older, and more *mature*, Brandon."

"Hey, man." Wade stood up and grinned, showcasing his perfect white teeth. "Wade. Houston."

Halley felt a shiver run down her spine. Wade had just met her brother. And apparently he'd met her mom. They were practically on their way down the aisle.

"So, sounds like someone's been kicking PlayStation butt around here." Wade glanced at the flat-screen TV on Tyler's bedroom wall. "Tekken. Good game."

Halley stood up and crossed her arms in a futile attempt to conceal the picture of Darth Vader on her shirt.

"You any good?" Halley asked skeptically.

"I haven't played in a while," Wade said, running his hand over his beautiful black fauxhawk so it flattened out and then sprang back to attention. "You know, I'm usually rehearsing these days."

"Right." Halley nodded. "Any new Wiggles songs on your set list?"

"Ha-ha," Wade said sarcastically, looking a little embarrassed but playful. "I'm actually here to grab the flyer for our *next* show. Sofee had to do something with her mom . . . or something."

"Oh, sure." Halley couldn't help but wonder if Sofee had sent Wade . . . or if he'd *volunteered*. "Um, follow me."

Halley felt like everything was moving in slow motion as she led the way to the stairs. In less than a minute, Wade would be in her bedroom. She tried to remember how she'd left it that morning. Had she made her bed? Were her dirty clothes on the floor? Oh god, had she hid her sketchbook of Wade portraits?

"Wow, so your mom really did work in the music industry." Wade stopped to stare at the gold and platinum records dedicated to Abigail Brandon.

"What, you thought I was lying?" Halley half-laughed, tossing her head back over her shoulder to smirk at Wade.

"No." Wade shook his head fervently. "I just—you know. It's cool, that's all."

Halley shrugged as she led Wade past her parents' minimalist, Japanese-inspired bedroom and two guestrooms— one decorated in earth tones, the other in deep, rich purples— that were connected by a massive black-and-white-tiled bathroom to her own, hopefully clean, room. She tentatively opened the door, silently praying that nothing deeply embarrassing was in plain sight. She peeked inside—*safe*.

Halley grabbed her brown leather messenger bag off her egg-shaped desk chair and rifled through it until she found the flyer she'd been working on. It was pretty impressive, if she did say so herself.

"So, this is the idea I had," Halley said, handing the flyer to Wade. It was a pen-and-ink drawing of the four bandmates, with *The Dead Romeos* written in script over their heads. The curlicues from the script swept around their heads and intertwined with the trees behind them. As he took it from her, their fingertips touched, sending a million little buzzing sparks of electricity shooting through her arms. His skin felt warm and soft, like Pucci's little belly. "I used some of the pictures from the photo shoot last week to make sure I got everyone's features right. I keep meaning to send those pictures to you guys, but I haven't had a chance yet. . . ."

"Jeez, Sofee was right," Wade said. "You're a really incredible artist."

"Oh. Thanks." Halley inhaled deeply, wanting to remember every detail of this moment forever: Wade's black T-shirt and the dark jeans, the black Docs and the way he smelled like salt water, coconut, and sandalwood. She already had most of his mesmerizing features memorized, of course, but at this close range, she noticed two tiny lines that crinkled around his eyes when he smiled. Were those new?

Wade walked over to the sliding-glass doors at the far end of her room and looked out across the lawn.

"Your house is really cool," Wade said. He raised his hand and traced what Halley could have sworn was the shape of a heart on the glass with his index finger. "That shed is awesome."

"Oh, yeah . . . it's my old playhouse," Halley murmured.

She'd been asking her dad to get rid of the old hut ever since she'd hit middle school, but he hadn't gotten around to it yet. As Halley stood and looked out over Wade's shoulder, she noticed Avalon's bedroom light was off. Courtney must not have picked her up from cheerleading practice yet.

Halley had a flash of brilliance. She had to get Wade in front of her house before Avalon got home! Seeing Halley with a new *boyfriend* would teach Avalon to shoot her mouth off about who could out-rock whom.

"Hey, you should take another look at the front of the house," Halley said, feeling amazingly inspired. "Especially the landscaping."

"Yeah?" Wade turned to face Halley and narrowed his onyx eyes. Every time he looked at her, she felt like he was hypnotizing her into adoring him even more. "Okay."

Halley guided Wade back downstairs and through the smoked-glass front door, onto the gray slate steps.

"So you kind of need to look at it from a certain angle to really get the whole design concept," Halley said, grabbing

Wade's shoulders and turning him so they were both facing the house. "If you look at it from here, you can see the ultra-modern influence in the lines. Do you see what I mean?" Halley waved her hand toward the curved walls that surrounded flower beds full of tropical trees and plants.

"What am I looking for again?" Wade sounded confused, which made Halley giggle inwardly since *she* wasn't exactly sure what she was trying to show him. All Halley knew as she cast a furtive glance down at Avalon's house was that she needed to keep Wade out front for as long as possible. At least until Avalon got home.

"Well, because the architecture is so postmodern, we really had to look for plants with super-specific kinds of lines and geometric shapes and stuff." Halley hoped she didn't sound too ridiculous, although continuing to confuse Wade would probably help her prolong this moment.

"Ohhh." Wade nodded, turning to face Halley and flashing a smile so hot, it could have melted the snow in Telluride. "I have no idea what you mean."

They locked eyes, and she finally felt completely at ease with him, like they were the perfect gray-camisole-and-black-cashmere-cardigan combination. Like they were soul mates. Like they could communicate without even speaking. And then they both burst out laughing.

"Okay, I don't actually know what I mean either," Halley said between laughs. She smiled and ran her hand over her hair, which was still sticky with Dr Pepper. Halley knew this was her moment to ask Wade if the Dead Romeos might want to play at her party next weekend. But that's when she spotted Courtney's blue VW Beetle convertible winding up the hill toward her house.

As the car turned into the Greenes' redbrick driveway, all Halley saw was Avalon's shiny blond ponytail in the passenger seat. At the last second, Avalon whipped her head around and looked straight at Halley. And Wade.

Even from a distance, Halley could see all the blood drain from Avalon's face and then a look of sheer I'm-gonna-puke shock. Avalon wasn't just jealous. She was *beyond* jealous. Seeing Avalon hurl over the side of Courtney's car would have just been icing on the cake of what was already pretty much the most perfect day of Halley's life. And Halley had always loved the icing best.

The official cyberzine of **Seaview Middle School**

QUIZ: What's Your Slumber Party Style?
by Style Snark A

posted: friday, 9/19, at 7:47 a.m.

If it's the weekend, it must be time for a pajama party! The good news is that your sleepwear is *hardly* limited to PJs. In fact, you've got after-hours ensemble options galore, and believe it or not, what you slip into says a lot about who you are. Answer the following questions to figure out what to pack in your overnight bag (and what to leave behind).*

1. **If there's one thing in life you live for, it's:**
   a) Shopping
   b) Rocking
   c) Jocking
   d) Reading

2. **The movies you like best are usually:**
   a) Romantic chick flicks
   b) Horror or psychological thrillers
   c) Action-adventures
   d) Comedies or cartoons

3. **Your favorite ice cream flavor is:**
   a) Strawberry
   b) Cherry Garcia
   c) Rocky Road
   d) Vanilla

4. **If you could kiss one celebrity, it would be:**
   a) Zac Efron
   b) Justin Timberlake
   c) Andy Roddick
   d) Adam Brody

5. **The best thing to do at slumber parties is:**
   a) Mani-pedis
   b) Tell scary stories and pull pranks
   c) Play games
   d) Sleep

If you answered mostly A's, you're GLAMTASTIC AND GIRLY.
While dressing up is always a good idea, you can probably
leave the over-the-top satin stuff at home and opt for a
matching cotton PJ set or a babydoll nightgown with a touch
of lace.

If you answered mostly B's, you're ARTSY AND UNUSUAL.
You're so into rocking and shocking, you might just wear a
cami and undies or even go more risqué—but your best bet
would be to keep your goodies covered up with a tank top and
boy shorts, at *least*. After all, it's a slumber party—not MTV
Spring Break!

If you answered mostly C's, you're SUPER-SPORTY.
Some people might call you a tomboy, especially if you decide
to sleep in the same oversized T-shirt you've been wearing all
week. Bring a fresh (and fairly fitted) top and shorts or some
high-end sweats, and you'll have an easier time shaking the
oh-so-undesirable slumberjack label.

If you answered mostly D's, you're BRAINY AND BASHFUL.
Dear Prudence, you may be too scared to show some skin,
but at least try undoing a button or two on that flannel
pajama top, and leave the long johns and fuzzy-footed
snugglebunnies under your Hello Kitty pillow—at home. Then
join in the fun . . . you might actually learn something from
your sassier and more experienced slumber-sisters.

* It should really go without saying, but *please* refrain from having
your sleepwear on when you arrive at the soiree itself; that just screams
"slumber party newbie."

Shop on,
Avalon Greene

Hey Avalon, if u pick out my pjs, I'll pick out yours.

posted by yeah_bro **on 9/19 at 7:53 a.m.**

OMG . . . did you hear what happened at Correy Halverson's house last weekend? Somebody with the initials KW fell asleep first and got her hand put in a bowl of warm water and, well . . . Huggies Overnights would have been helpful that evening. SO TRAGIQUE!

posted by luv2gossip **on 9/19 at 7:55 a.m.**

Awesome quiz! I didn't know I was "artsy and unusual"—but I do usually go a little too HFMOG (hot-for-my-own-good!) at pj parties. Not anymore . . . Thank U. xoxo

posted by veepme **on 9/19 at 8:04 a.m.**

No rest for the cheery

 tanding in her new red Michael Stars babydoll tank and cropped black leggings, Avalon scanned the living room one last time to make sure everything was ready. The game could not have gone better—even if Avalon didn't have her real uniform yet. She hoped the rest of the evening would go as well, solidifying her as one of the team.

The big velvet sofas were pulled out of the way so they framed the sunken living room, creating plenty of space on the sage-colored Moroccan carpet for all ten girls to lay out their sleeping bags. The dark leather coffee table in the middle of the rug was overflowing with brightly colored bowls full of Milk Duds, Baked Doritos, and popcorn, as well as a platter of fresh-cut veggies, and Avalon's favorite sour cream–and–dill dip. Avalon had already made sure the fridge was stocked with SmartWater and caffeine-free diet soda and that there were no signs of Red Bull anywhere.

Avalon grabbed a stack of magazines—including *Us Weekly, People, Vogue, Lucky*, and her latest obsession, *American Cheerleader*—from a red suede magazine rack and scattered them around the rug. Then she walked over to the light switches in the domed foyer and dimmed the recessed lights overhead so the golden-taupe sponge-painted walls took on an even warmer glow.

Finally, she found the remote between tubs of Red Vines on the table, pressed a button, and began scrolling through shows on the flat-screen plasma TV above the white stone fireplace. What would be appropriate viewing for a party with the pep squad? MTV, E!, VH1? Comedy Central, the CW, ESPN? None of them sounded exactly right, so Avalon turned off the TV and opted for music instead.

She opened the doors of the ornate entertainment center and shuffled through the playlists on her iPod—gymtastics (time to delete that one), beach jams, workout mix, BFF'ed (another to delete), sobfest, giddy-up, tennis camp tracks, cheer-a-licious—until she found the one she was looking for: slumber-ation. But as Pink began pumping out of the built-in ceiling speakers, Avalon panicked. What if Brianna felt the lyrics were offensive or inappropriate? What if Sydney laughed at Avalon's taste in music? Avalon decided to just play her entire Kelly Clarkson playlist. *Everybody* liked Kelly, right?

Avalon couldn't remember the last time she'd been this nervous before a slumber party. Then again, she'd never thrown one without Halley as her co-planner. Of course, after seeing Halley with Wade in front of her house yesterday, Avalon was almost relieved they were no longer friends. Okay, maybe a little jealous Halley had a boyfriend—even if it was *Wade*—but *mostly* relieved. Before long, Halley would have an eyebrow piercing and a pair of cowboy boots for every day of the week. Halley's true colors had finally come out, and they obviously clashed with Avalon's *big-time*.

Just as Avalon was making a quick mental list of activities and conversation topics for the evening (practicing routines, spa treatments, Oprah), the doorbell rang.

"Hey!" Brianna gave Avalon a crushing, heartfelt hug when she opened the door. "You look awesome."

"So do you." Avalon smiled at Brianna's distressed pink sweats. "Love the sweats. Juicy?"

"I don't know," Brianna said, reaching behind her neck to pull out the tag.

"Scrapbook," Avalon read the label, shaking her head at how effortlessly chic Brianna was. "Supercute." Within twenty minutes, the rest of the squad had arrived, and everyone was dancing around the living room to "Since U Been Gone." Avalon finally felt like she belonged. Like she was one of them. Brianna didn't seem to mind that the girls might exhaust themselves with too much partying, and even Sydney seemed to be warming up. She and Avalon actually bonded over their excitement for the mani-pedi part of the evening.

"That's my favorite, too!" Avalon squealed, dragging Sydney into the downstairs bathroom to show her the professional pink cosmetics case she had full of every kind of nail polish, from dark OPI reds to shimmery Hard Candy pastels. They decided they'd partner up for the "spa-mazing" portion of the evening later on.

"You know, I'm really glad you're on the squad," Sydney said softly, her violet eyes sparkling in the dim light of the bathroom.

"Thanks." Avalon grinned, breathing in the scent of the sweet jasmine candles that were burning in wrought-iron sconces on either side of the oval bathroom mirror. Had she completely misjudged Sydney? She felt a pang of guilt for all the mean thoughts she'd had about her. "I am, too!"

Avalon and Sydney giggled and gave each other a quick hug. When they got back into the living room, Brianna announced that they should practice some cheers in the backyard. "We can show you the flashlight routine we made up at camp over the summer," Sydney told Avalon.

Avalon ran into the garage to grab a boxful of blue flashlights from the family's earthquake emergency trunk and led the girls outside. Even though Avalon had turned off all the lights—"for the full flashlight effect"—it seemed like every last lamp in the Brandons' house was on, illuminating both adjacent yards. Avalon looked up and saw the paper lanterns glowing through the glass doors of Halley's bedroom.

She dashed inside to get her iPod. As long as they were practicing, she wanted to make sure Halley could hear absolutely everything she was missing.

I'll see your boyfriend and raise you nine cheerleaders!

Even though the air was crisp and slightly chilly, Avalon felt warm inside. She watched the squad show off the routines they'd done on Wake the Spirit Night at cheer camp, and then joined them for a bunch of the ones she already knew. They were all yelling as loudly as they possibly could, falling onto the cool, soft grass as they worked on pyramids and tumbling passes while Pink's "Stupid Girls" blared over the SoundDock speakers.

They all begged Avalon to teach them her famous "Crazy V" tumbling combination, which everyone had been calling "the Avalon" since Wednesday. But she kept losing it right as she was going from the second back-handspring into the back tuck. As Avalon lay in the grass, she heard Pucci's familiar bark. She looked up to see Halley and the puppy standing on the other side of the wooden fence.

"Hey!" Halley yelled, trying to stop Pucci from jumping up on the gate to get to the Greenes' yard.

Pucci bounded over to Avalon and slobbered her with wet kisses, obviously letting her know which parent she preferred.

"Oh, hey, guys, how's it going?" Halley flashed an awkward

smile, as if she hadn't heard them cheering for the past half hour. "What are you all doing here?"

"Postgame slumber party," Brianna explained, wiping her forehead with the back of her hand. "Avalon was just trying to teach us this amazing tumbling pass she does, but it's driving us all insane."

"Oh," Halley said, kicking her white Nike sneakers into the lawn. "What's the pass?"

"Round off, two back-handsprings, back tuck, splits, 'Go, Lions!'" Avalon said flatly, mimicking the V-pose Halley always made with her arms when she mocked cheerleading.

"Like this?" Halley took a running start and executed the pass perfectly. "Go, Lions!"

"Wow, you did it on the first try!" Andi enthused. The little brunette looked like she was going to jump into Halley's arms.

"Do it again, Hal," Tanya said.

"Oh, hey, Tanya." Halley smiled at her muscular tennis teammate. They'd been temporary doubles partners in sixth grade when Avalon sprained her ankle.

Halley did the tumbling pass three more times, giving Avalon and the other cheerleaders a chance to try again after her. It had officially turned into a tumble-off, and Avalon hated to admit that Halley appeared to be winning.

"How do you *do* that?" asked Saffron and Samantha Boswell incredulously. Most people referred to them as "the Roswell Twins" because they almost looked like identical aliens with their tall, lanky bodies, close-cropped brown hair, and enormous amber eyes.

"I don't know." Halley shrugged, wiping her hands on her faded navy sweatpants. "You just do it."

Avalon shivered, hugging her arms around her chest. "Jeez, it's really getting cold out here, isn't it?" Avalon finally asked, glancing around at the squad members. "Maybe we should head inside."

"Hey, Halley, you should come inside, too," Andi said, spraying Halley with her *s*.

Avalon felt like the grass beneath her had just turned to quicksand and she was slowly sinking into a pit of despair. She reached out and grabbed Pucci's red-and-yellow scarf, holding on to it for dear life, and somehow managed to plaster a smile on her face.

"Oh, thanks," Halley said, narrowing her eyes in Avalon's direction. "But I've got plans."

Avalon stormed back to the house with her squadmates following closely behind. She couldn't decide if she was:

1. Relieved that Halley had turned down Andi's invitation.
2. Concerned that Halley might actually have better things to do.
3. Annoyed that her attempt to make Halley jealous had backfired so horribly.

Avalon decided on all of the above, and was then triple-irritated as she realized that between the Wade incident and tonight's tumbling pass-off, she and Halley were currently tied in the better-off-without-you war.

Well, Avalon knew exactly how to step up her game. After all, she had *developed* certain qualities that were impossible to ignore. And by the time her spa-mazing dark purple nail polish had dried later that night, the plan would already be in motion.

SCHOOL NEWS | HEALTH | SPORTS | ENTERTAINMENT | **COMPETITION**

POLL: What Were You Wearing When—?
by Style Snark B

posted: monday, 9/22, at 7:14 a.m.

Have you ever had one of those days when everything just fell into place—your crush finally noticed you, you won your first big game, aced a test you were super-worried about, or came up with the perfect comeback in a heated debate? Those are the moments you want to remember forever, and a great way to do that is by taking a mental photograph of how you looked at the time. You might even save the entire ensemble you were wearing in a memory box somewhere. (Sounds dorky, but hey—most brides do it with wedding gowns, right?) So, here's the question:

What was the best day of your life, what happened, and what were you wearing?

Let everyone know by posting below!

Word to your closet,

Halley Brandon

OMG . . . I was wearing a strapless Free People floral top over my new True Religion stretch skinny jeans and red suede Miss Sixty platforms, shopping at Horton Plaza, when the hottest guy EVER said hi to me. By the next day we were IMing nonstop and he eventually became my BF. Then he cheated on me and I dumped him . . . but I'm still in love with my outfit from that day! Boys let you down, clothes don't. ☺

posted by slave2fashun **on 9/22 at 7:29 a.m.**

Betsey Johnson rosebud-print bikini . . . beach party, bonfire, cute boys, awesome tunes, first kiss . . . 'nuff said. AHHHHHH!

posted by madameprez **on 9/22 at 7:54 a.m.**

I was wearing my football uniform and we DOMINATED! Seaview Middle School football RULES!

posted by whosURdaddy **on 9/22 at 8:12 a.m.**

If I told you, then I'd have to kill u.

posted by fourstrikes **on 9/22 at 8:14 a.m.**

Rack 'n' roll

On Monday, Halley was mere yards away from Wade and the Dead Romeos—the only invited guest to their afternoon rehearsal. Again. She traced the outline of a heart on the knee of her black L.A.M.B. sailor-front pants with a silver-painted fingernail and bobbed her head along to the slow beat of the song. Sure, the musical-note-shaped chairs were made of hard and totally uncomfortable plastic, but a slightly numbing butt-cramp didn't bother Halley in the least.

The mood of the song was mellow, but Halley's insides were slam-dancing in a mosh pit. In fact, ever since Thursday at 5:17 p.m., Halley had been playing scenes from Wade's visit to her house again . . . and again . . . and again in her head. Just for fun, she would occasionally throw in a visual of Avalon staring in shock out Courtney's car window or recall the looks on the faces of the cheerleaders when Halley kept showing them how a tumbling pass was really done.

When the song ended, Sofee leaned her red guitar on its metal stand and stepped down from the small square platform stage at the front of the room. She looked particularly rocker-chic today, with a black knit cap pulled down over her long platinum-streaked dark curls. She'd also layered ripped denim shorts over black tights and a black short-sleeved T-shirt over a long-sleeved gray hoodie. Avalon would have No'ed the entire thing, which made Halley like it even more.

"So, what'd you think?" Sofee asked, picking a stray hair off Halley's gray-and-black striped tunic.

Halley smiled her thanks for the hair-removal help. "You guys sound better every time I hear you."

"That's pretty huge coming from *you*!" Mason yelled at Halley from behind his drum kit as if she were sitting several rows farther away than she actually was.

"What do you mean?" Halley asked Mason somewhat nonchalantly, hoping he was about to divulge a juicy piece of information about Wade's innermost feelings for her.

"Wade told us about all your gold plaques!" Mason squealed. That was juicy enough for Halley. Wade had been talking about a wall in *her house* with the guys in *his band*! It was practically dude-speak for *I love her*.

"They're her *mom*'s plaques, you doof," Evan said, rolling his eyes and glancing over at Halley before going back to turning one of the silver knobs on the end of his bass.

Meanwhile, Wade had yet to look up.

"Wade also said he thinks your house is awesome," Sofee said, pulling at a grid of thick white threads that were stretched between one of the smaller holes in her faded jean shorts.

Wade finally looked up and focused his eyes on Halley's.

Swoon.

He nodded his head. "I told them all about the postmodern lines of the palm trees."

Double swoon.

It was the same quasi-nonsense she'd used when she was trying to show him off to Avalon.

"Huh?" Mason asked, tossing a drumstick in the air and shocking himself by actually catching it.

"Yeah, what are you *talking* about?" Sofee added, raising one perfectly arched eyebrow.

"Nothing." Wade laughed. Halley smiled conspiratorially. They had an inside joke that nobody in the band could figure out. How awesome was *that*?

"Whatever." Sofee exhaled loudly through her nose, causing the tiny diamond stud in it to tremble. She picked up her army satchel from the empty seat to her right and began rummaging around inside it until she found her iPhone, then she started typing a text message.

"What I *did* tell them," Wade said, running his index finger along the neckband of his gray Foo Fighters T-shirt, "is that your backyard would be the perfect place to shoot our first video."

"Oh, yeah?" Halley gave Wade a flirty-quizzical look.

"Yeah, and I was thinking you might even want to shoot it for us," Wade added with a gleam in his dark eyes. "Those pictures you e-mailed us on Friday night were pretty cool. How are you with a video camera?"

"I'm okay." Halley looked at Sofee out of the corner of her eye for backup, but Sofee was checking messages on her iPhone now and seemed almost completely oblivious to the conversation. "I mean, I'm actually the official gymnastics videographer . . . so, you know, I'm getting *pretty* good at shooting and cutting and splicing and stuff."

"I told you guys," Wade said, looking from Sofee to Evan to Mason. "Halley's our girl."

Halley hit a mental PAUSE button. Our girl? As far as Halley was concerned, he had just announced she was *his* girl—as in girl*friend*.

She wanted to do cartwheels and back-handsprings all through the hallways of the main SMS building, down the brick path, past the villas, and out to the football field, where she'd kick grass up into Avalon's face. But instead, she just said, "Absolutely."

"How about tomorrow after school?"

Video concepts and funky quick-cut edit techniques flashed through Halley's mind. She could almost see herself accepting one MTV VMA after another. And how impressed would Wade be with her then? Oh! And she could premiere the video at the party at Nate's! She couldn't wait to see Wade's reaction—and Avalon's. Of course, she still had to ask the Dead Romeos to play.

Just then the squeak of the music room door opening broke Halley out of her mental celebration. Everyone turned to identify the newcomer. Halley's jaw dropped at the sight of her.

Avalon's nails were painted purple, and she wore a skin-tight black T-shirt with THE RAMONES written in big red letters that were stretched even bigger because of where they were positioned: right on Avalon's chest.

"Are you lost?" Halley tossed her head so her long dark hair fell behind her shoulders.

"Oh, hey, Halley," Avalon replied, walking directly over to Wade, where she extended her arm confidently. "Hi, I'm Avalon. Greene."

"Hey," Wade said, shaking Avalon's hand and then shoving his hand in the back pocket of his dark-wash jeans.

Halley's pulse pounded in her temples. Not only had Avalon just made flesh-on-flesh contact with *her* Dead Romeo, but Wade was staring directly at Avalon's chest. Halley tried to convince herself that he was just a fan of the Ramones, but as

Avalon said hi to Evan and Mason, and Halley saw where *their* eyes were focused, she couldn't delude herself any longer.

"Hey, Avalon, I'm Sofee. *Hughes*," Sofee sneered, getting up from her seat as she shot a half-amused, half-incredulous look back at Halley.

Avalon laughed. "Ha, ha." Then she looked at each of the boys with a perky little grin she must have learned from the cheer*followers*. "We know each other."

Sofee sighed and sat back down. "So what brings you to our little practice space today?"

"I just wanted to come and meet the band that would be playing *our* party this weekend." Avalon sat down next to Halley and draped her arm around her shoulders.

Halley was so frozen by the whole scene that she couldn't even wriggle away.

Sofee looked at Halley and uttered a one-word question: "Party?"

"Oh, yeah." Halley nodded at Sofee and then glanced at the boys. "I've been meaning to ask if you guys wanted to play—at Nate's—on Saturday—but I kept forgetting—and I was actually just about to tell you—"

"Hey, we'd love to come to your party," Wade interjected almost giddily, flashing a big smile at . . .

The Ramones.

"Yeah, that sounds *awesome*!" Mason yelled to . . .

The Ramones.

"I'm all about parties," Evan added quietly to . . .

The Ramones.

Getting Wade to come to the party should have felt like a major victory. But instead, Halley got a distinct sense that her winning streak was about to end.

EXCLUSIVE INTERVIEW!
If These Clothes Could Talk
by Style Snark A

posted: tuesday, 9/23, at 7:43 a.m.

Ever wondered what it's like to hang in the closets of some of the best-dressed peeps in school? Well, here, for the first time ever, we bring you this exclusive interview with—yes, you guessed it—some of the actual clothes and accessories belonging to none other than Style Snark B! Enjoy . . .

> **SSA: What's the best thing about being a part of Style Snark B's *awesome* wardrobe?**
>
> **FUGG SUEDE BOOTS:** The fact that she wears us, even though everyone else thinks we're passé. Seriously, we feel *so* loved by her.

SSA: Well, what's the worst thing about being a part of her wardrobe, then?

BCBG SWEATER FROM LAST SEASON: Honestly? I have to say she totally used me. She wore me all of *one* time, even though she swore she loved me when she first tried me on. I've been wadded up in the back of a drawer with a bunch of other sweaters for *months* now . . . and I never even got sent to the cleaners.

SSA: If there's one thing you'd change about SSB's closet, what would it be?

LOUIS VUITTON KNOCKOFF CLUTCH: Uh, all those nasty-looking music T-shirts she got from her mom. Does she really think she's fooling anyone with those?

SSA: Well, no offense, but you're a fake yourself. Don't you have any sympathy for the wannabes?

FAKE LOUIS: No comment.

And there you have it! Apparently SSB's closet has been keeping as many secrets as Victoria . . . until now. ☺

Shop on,
Avalon Greene

Oh no you DIDN'T! Style Snark A, u r a very bad girl. Me likey.

posted by veepme **on 9/23 at 7:50 a.m.**

So if the devil wears Prada, what does SSA wear? Cuz this is one eeevil column. Poor B. Not nice . . . but fug-in' funny!

posted by luv2gossip **on 9/23 at 7:58 a.m.**

Dude, this column is ridiculous . . . in a good way, natch. LUV IT! Sorry SSB.

posted by hotterthanU **on 9/23 at 8:07 a.m.**

Breaking news

For the second Tuesday in a row, Avalon found her-self sitting in the journalism villa with Halley during lunch. But this time, they weren't alone. Miss Frey had called them in for a meeting about the *Daily* column competition.

"Well, thanks for coming in during your lunch break," Miss Frey said, running a hand over her glossy dark hair, which skimmed her shoulders with an upflip at the ends.

"No problem." Avalon gazed at her teacher, who could not have been more of a Yes today in her brightly colored kimono top and skinny jeans—which were actually almost identical to Avalon's.

"Sure." Halley smiled, too, and kept her eyes focused straight ahead at Miss Frey.

"I've got some good news and some bad news," Miss Frey continued.

Avalon held her breath and silently hoped Miss Frey would point out how ridiculous it was for Halley to try to give fashion advice to *anybody*, particularly in light of today's faded blue R.E.M. T-shirt, ripped jeans, and heinous black boots.

"Good news first," Miss Frey said, taking off her dark-rimmed glasses. "Your column competition posts are generating more Web traffic than the *Daily* has ever seen. You've clearly hit a nerve with the school, and the students can't get enough of you."

For about a half second, Avalon and Halley locked eyes and shared a silent victory grin. Then, just as quickly, they looked away.

"Now for the bad news." Miss Frey dropped her gaze and ran her fingers side-to-side along the black leather ink blotter on her desk. Her dark red lips were in a tight, awkward smile, and her pale blue eyes looked like watery tide pools. "I'm concerned by how disparaging you've been in some of your columns—to your classmates, and especially to each other."

Avalon looked down at the dark wood surface of her desk and felt a hot, prickling sensation start in her hands and then spread through her body.

"I'm as ambitious as the next girl," Miss Frey continued. "But *no* competition is worth the sort of antagonism you two are displaying."

Avalon felt like she was in a stranglehold. She didn't think the columns had been *that* bad. . . . She wanted to speak up, to tell Miss Frey she was sorry or that they had just been trying to add a little drama to the *Daily* and boost interest in the magazine. But Halley's clear, controlled voice cut through the silence.

"You're right, Miss Frey," Halley said, drumming her silver-painted fingernails on her desk—each tap sounded like a tiny spear jabbing into Avalon's back. "We really should try to be more constructive."

"I'm glad you feel that way, Halley." Miss Frey's face brightened as she stood up and walked around to the front of her desk. "The thing is, if you can't be respectful of your readers, how can you expect them to treat *you* with respect?"

"We can't," Halley declared, again cutting Avalon off at the pass. Avalon turned her head and narrowed her eyes at Halley. "But we've still got time to turn things around, right?"

"Yes, Halley," Miss Frey said. "And I really hope you'll do that. Otherwise, I might be forced to disqualify you."

"No!" Avalon slammed her palms down on her desk, startling even herself. "I mean, you wouldn't really have to do *that*, would you?"

"I hope not," Miss Frey said, tilting her head to one side and looking quizzically at Avalon. "Up until today, I was going to give you two the benefit of the doubt—write it all off as edgy snarkasm."

Avalon smiled. That's right, she was just being snarkastic. That's all. The things she said weren't intended as anything but lighthearted jabs.

Really.

"But your column this morning was particularly hurtful," Miss Frey continued, narrowing her eyes at Avalon and jolting her back to reality. "So please just keep that in mind and think about how your words are reflecting on the *Daily*—not to mention on *yourselves*. And please also remember that you entered this competition *together*. That means you win together or you lose together."

"Don't worry, Miss Frey," Halley chimed in again, totally unfazed. "We'll be on our best behavior from now on."

"Great," Miss Frey said, turning and walking around to the back of her desk, where she bent down to pick up her brown Coach tote. "And you're on the same page with that, Avalon?"

"Yeah." Avalon nodded her head firmly and blinked back the tears stinging her eyes. This meeting was practically all her fault. "Of course."

"Glad to hear it." Miss Frey smiled, folding her glasses into a case and popping them in her bag, then sliding on her Dior shades. "Well, I'm starving. Why don't you go get some lunch while you still have time, and I'll see you tomorrow?"

Halley quickly grabbed her messenger bag off the floor and followed Miss Frey out without even looking back.

Avalon felt like a broken mirror—unlucky and totally shattered. She *had* to come up with a way to redeem herself. Avalon walked over to sit at the iMac she used to share with Halley. She clicked to the SMS's site and scrolled through her latest column comments. They loved her snarktastic attack on Halley—some people were even asking for Halley to write a response in her next column. And that gave Avalon an idea.

Just shoot me

*H*alley lay on her stomach in her backyard, shooting the final scene for the Dead Romeos' very first video. It was the perfect distraction from Avalon's morning column and the talk with Miss Frey at lunchtime. All day at school, people had pretended to interview Halley's clothes.

"Hello, Mr. T-shirt, how do you feel about Halley today?"

Because *that* was clever. . . .

The entire band was jumping around on the slightly sloped roof of Halley's old wooden playhouse. Halley silently thanked her dad for spending so many mornings surfing instead of tearing the thing down. As far as Halley was concerned, it was pretty much a national landmark now.

With the Dead Romeos' "What's in a Name" blaring through Halley's portable stereo, the band pretended to sing and play along. Halley shot another take of the band, and was filled with the same elated feeling she'd had yesterday afternoon—prior to the arrival of Maliboob Barbie. The fact that Wade was in *her* yard and had asked her to shoot *his* video had to mean more than a few hormonal minutes of ogling Avalon's chest, right?

"Yeah! We're *rock stars*!" Mason yelled as the song ended. He was sitting on Halley's old pink princess stool behind his sparkly blue drum kit, both of which were perched precariously on the flattest part of the playhouse roof.

As Wade leapt down to the ground, followed by the rest of the band, Halley got up from the grass and turned to steal a quick glance over the picket fence dividing her yard from Avalon's. She looked up at the arched picture window of Avalon's room just in time to see a shadowy figure disappear from view.

Ha!

"So, is that a wrap or what?" Wade asked, walking over to Halley as he wiped the back of his hand across his glowing forehead.

Halley was eternally amazed by how Wade got even better looking with each passing day. He'd changed his faux-hawk slightly; it was a little messier and less spiky, making his face seem softer and his dark eyes even more intense. Meanwhile, the whole band had gone with a dressed-up punk rock look, complete with white button-down oxfords and black ties for the boys and a metallic red minidress with black knee-high boots for Sofee. It was all too perfect for words.

"Yeah." Halley nodded, playfully holding the camera away from Wade when he tried to grab it out of her hands. "But you can't see the footage till I've put together a *flawless* video!"

"How could it be anything *but* flawless with music gods like us in it?" Mason screamed and punched Evan. Halley wasn't sure if Evan winced from the punch or Mason's extreme volume.

"Uh, correction: gods and *goddesses*." Sofee walked up between the drummer and bass player, wrapping her arms around them and grinning. Then she leaned toward Halley and Wade. "Seriously, though, do you think you can make something out of all that?"

"Absolutely," Halley said, turning when she heard a familiar bark and saw Pucci bounding through the gate with Avalon chasing after her.

Halley's stomach tightened up. How dare Avalon come over after this morning's column! And P.S., could she be any more obvious? After all, Halley had done the same thing Friday night when she'd wanted to interrupt Avalon's slumber party with the pep squad. And P.P.S., it was totally Halley's day for Pucci custody. How did Avalon even get her hands on the puppy?

"*Heyyyy,*" Avalon cooed, stopping short in front of Halley and Wade, apparently forgetting all about chasing after Pucci, who had decided to sniff around the playhouse.

Halley stared down at the grass. She'd already seen enough of Avalon in the tight white T-shirt with neon green letters spelling WHAM! across the chest. Besides, she figured if she kept her eyes averted, she wouldn't have to watch Wade coming down with another case of the boobonic plague.

"Hey!" Halley heard Mason practically drooling. "Avalon, right? Party girl! Woo hoo!"

"Um, yeah," Avalon said with hesitation in her voice.

Halley couldn't take it any longer. She *had* to see what Wade was doing.

But when she looked up, she saw that he and Sofee had wandered back over to the playhouse to get their equipment. Halley shrugged smugly at Avalon.

And she would have felt completely confident—except Halley recognized the faint glimmer of mischief in Avalon's brown eyes. She knew her ex-bestie the way no one else could—and she knew, without a doubt, that the girl was up to *something*.

The official cyberzine of **Seaview Middle School**

ANOTHER EXCLUSIVE!
If These Clothes Could Talk, 2
by Style Snark B

posted: wednesday, 9/24, at 7:01 a.m.

Given the enthusiastic responses to yesterday's interview, it seemed only fitting that we get an inside glimpse into how it feels to hang in Style Snark A's closet. This might just be the most revealing thing to hit campus since Heather Ramos's tube top tragedy at last year's midwinter formal.

SSB: Tell us something we'd *never* expect to hear about Style Snark A.

HIDEOUS BLUE BABYDOLL TOP: She's abusive! When she took one look in the mirror, she practically ripped me off. Then she threw me on the ground and kicked me—like it was *my* fault that I didn't fit her anymore. Someone should call style protective services.

SSB: Do you really think she intentionally meant to hurt you?

DKNY CAMI: Of course, darling. Have you seen the way she stretches me mercilessly over her chest? I mean, come on: Accept that you've got 'em and buy a bigger size already.

SSB: Maybe she just thinks tight clothes are more flattering.

CALVIN DENIM MINI: You can say that again!

SSB: Well, are there any pluses to hanging in Style Snark A's closet?

PINK CASHMERE CARDIGAN: None come to mind at the moment.

Ouch! Sounds like it's time for Style Snark A to undergo an extreme makeover of some sort. . . .

Word to your closet,
Halley Brandon

COMMENTS (227)

Whoa! Now we just need to know: Are her boobs real or not?
posted by luv2gossip **on 9/24 at 7:13 a.m.**

Ha . . . I dunno if I feel worse for SSA or her DKNY cami. ☺
posted by rockgirrrl **on 9/24 at 7:32 a.m.**

Snark-o-rama!
posted by fembot95 **on 9/24 at 7:49 a.m.**

I think snarka can take snarkb in a boxing match. But my $s
still on mark cohen's clumn to win.
posted by tuffprincess **on 9/24 at 8:52 a.m.**

Rise and whine

"Halley Amelia Brandon!"

Halley pulled her electric toothbrush from her lips and stared at her reflection in the bathroom mirror. Was her mom really calling her by all three of her names at 7:40 a.m. on a Wednesday?

"Halley!"

Well that answered that. Halley spat out her toothpaste in the porcelain sink and followed her mother's voice down the hall and to her parents' bedroom.

Abigail was leaning back against the headboard of her white platform bed. She set the latest issue of *Entertainment Weekly* down on the tiny bedside table as her pale blue eyes settled on Halley. "We need to talk."

"Sure," Halley agreed, sinking into the edge of the white silk duvet. "What's up?"

"Well." Abigail sighed, her tone as muted as the soft light coming from two Asian-style pillar floor lamps. "I just got a call from Miss Frey."

"Uh-huh?" Halley couldn't imagine why Miss Frey would have called so early in the morning.

"Apparently you were given a pretty stern warning yesterday?" Abigail adjusted a big white pillow behind her back and crossed her long slender legs, clad in oversize cotton pajama bottoms.

"Yup." Halley nodded. "But I think we're all good now."

"Think again, *Style Snark B*. I read what you wrote about Avalon this morning, and I'm pretty shocked you'd make fun of her that way."

"What—?" Halley brushed aside a wisp of wavy brown hair that had managed to escape from her low ponytail and sat up tall on the edge of her parents' bed. She hadn't posted anything on the column competition since her "What were you wearing?" poll on Monday. She was planning on writing this morning's column while she ate breakfast—she'd been too busy with the video and homework to write it last night.

Halley batted her heavily lashed blue eyes as she stood up and straightened the hem of her short-sleeved Lucky camo hoodie over her dark skinny jeans. "But I haven't written this morning's column yet."

"Well, then, who did?" Abigail challenged. "Because *someone* had some pretty nasty things to say about Avalon."

"I don't—" Then Halley stopped. You had to log in to post a column, and the only other person who had a log-in ID for the *Daily* column-competition fashion page was . . . *Avalon.*

Halley lowered her head and looked up at Abigail with her most apologetic, give-me-another-chance eyes. "I'll figure out a way to make it right."

"Good . . ." Abigail's voice trailed off as Halley made a beeline for her room.

Halley sat down and turned on her iMac, immediately logging in to the *Daily* Web site. She read Avalon's post and several old columns until she found what she was looking for.

After that, it didn't take long for Halley to compose the perfect solution.

Coming Out of the Closet
by the Style Snarks

posted: thursday, 9/25, at 7:02 a.m.

Okay, everyone. Confession time. The Style Snarks have been caught in the act of snarking on each other, and we have no choice at this point but to make up and come clean on some of our previous posts. As fun as it's probably been for you to watch our antics in such a public forum, all good things must come to an end. And so, in the interest of full disclosure and making peace, we're going to provide the answers that inquiring minds want to know. Here we go!

1. Style Snark A does *not* abuse her clothes. When she's in hate with something, she simply boxes it up (carefully) and ships it off to Buffalo Exchange in Pacific Beach. (Check it out; maybe you'll get the opportunity to purchase one of her castoffs!)

2. Style Snark B's boots aren't really scary; Style Snark A was just a little jealous that she didn't wear them first.

3. Style Snark A really does recommend wearing tight clothes and short skirts. "They're flirtatiously feminine and scandalously sassy," she says. ☺

4. Style Snark B's LV clutch is real. It was a birthday gift from Style Snark A!

5. Style Snark A's blue babydoll tee wasn't really hideous, just a little snug up top.

6. Style Snark B's BCBG sweater from last season was actually kind of cute.

7. Were Style Snark A's boobs really the work of a team of highly skilled plastic surgeons? Here's a hint: The answer begins with "Obvi." ☺

8. Style Snark B has not been surgically altered in any way (duh!).

We hope that clears up any confusion our preceding columns may have caused. We're back on track now and ready to provide you with the authoritative attire advice for whatever clothing conundrums confound you.

Word to your closet,   Shop on,

Halley Brandon   *Avalon Greene*

OMG! I knew they weren't real! I just can't believe you finally admitted it.

posted by luv2gossip **on 9/25 at 7:30 a.m.**

Still seems like there's some snarking going on here. I'm not sure I'm buying the whole kiss-and-make-up thing. I guess time will tell.

posted by eternalpessimist **on 9/25 at 7:41 a.m.**

Hey! I think I have one of your old sweaters from Buffalo Exchange. Did U sell them that teal Free People cardigan U used to wear? Could it b I actually own a Style Snark original?!

posted by fuglybettie **on 9/25 at 7:52 a.m.**

YAY! So glad U R being nice to each other again, cuz I adore U both!

posted by cheeriously **on 9/25 at 8:02 a.m.**

The setup

$\mathcal{A}$ valon adjusted her favorite black D&G sunglasses to keep the salty sea breeze from stinging her eyes as she trudged toward one of the volleyball courts at La Jolla Shores. Once again, The Moms had decided to surprise their daughters after school. Didn't Constance have someone to prosecute or something? And if sharing a ride home weren't bad enough, The Moms had driven them all down to the beach for a predinner game to finalize plans for the party and just "have some fun together!"

Avalon cringed. "Fun" no longer had any part of time spent with Halley. Pain . . . misery . . . torture, yes. Fun, no. *Especially* after the stunt Halley had pulled in their *Daily* column this morning, to which she'd signed Avalon's name. It was going to take some major damage control to undo all the lies Halley had posted about her.

The beach was surprisingly crowded for a Thursday. Sun-worshippers were trying to score a few last rays, at least a dozen surfers bobbed up and down on the frothy white caps of the Pacific, and a large family was enjoying a late-afternoon picnic at the base of the rocky cliffs that towered above the sand. Avalon saw two women chasing after their little girls—one blonde, one brunette—and she couldn't help but remember the happier times she and Halley had spent with their own moms in that exact spot. And yet here they were, expected to go through the same old motions as if the past two weeks of total-friendship-destruction had never happened.

"All right, here's the plan," Constance announced, kicking off her beige leather sandals next to the post that held one end of the high, white net. "We thought we'd mix things up a little and play moms against daughters."

Avalon and Halley both let out audible groans. The tradition had always been the Greenes versus the Brandons. And as much as Avalon had been dreading doing anything with Halley today, she'd at least been hoping to pummel her in a few straight sets.

"Listen," Abigail said, her voice sounding a lot sterner than she looked in her baby-blue tank and black yoga pants. "We're getting a little tired of all this fighting. You're best friends and you're having a party this weekend to celebrate that."

"Unless, that is ... you can't work together and win today's game," Constance chimed in matter-of-factly, tucking her short platinum hair behind her ears and adjusting her sunglasses.

"Meaning what?" Avalon couldn't believe what she was hearing.

"Meaning we're playing for the party." The tight smile on Constance's bright red lips told the girls she meant business. "If you lose, there won't be one."

"But"—Abigail grinned—"if you can work as a team, it's still on."

"And that's not all," Constance continued, as if she had just decided to hawk her wares on an infomercial.

"You're kidding, right?" Halley looked as horrified as Avalon felt.

"Not even a little," Constance said just as Abigail replied with, "Nope."

Clearly The Moms had been watching too much of *The Amazing Race*.

Avalon and Halley stared after The Moms as they walked to the other side of the court. Avalon bit her glossed lip, willing Halley to speak first. A seagull flew overhead and squawked.

"I like your hoodie," Halley finally offered, looking Avalon directly in the eye.

"Thanks," Avalon said, encouraged as she pulled off her

193

Truly Madly Deeply rainbow-striped sweatshirt to reveal a formfitting red sports tank. But as much as she wanted the party, she couldn't resist a jab: "And what do you think of my Dr. 90210s?"

"Those aren't *real*?!" Halley asked, lowering her eyes to Avalon's chest and half-smiling. "But they look so natural."

"That's not what I read." Avalon sneered, although she really wanted to giggle along with her best—er, old friend.

"Sorry about that." Halley shrugged as she got to her feet and took her position near the front of the net. "But you kind of asked for it."

Avalon tossed her blond ponytail and walked to the back corner of the volleyball court, trying to figure out her next move.

"Rally for service!" Constance yelled, hitting the neon orange volleyball over the net. Halley and Avalon both went for it at once and nearly slammed into each other as the ball landed on the sand in the middle of their side of the court.

"Our serve," Abigail cheered. "Come on, girls—teamwork!"

"We've gotta make this work," Avalon insisted as she picked up the ball off the sand and tossed it under the net to The Moms. "Right?"

"Right." Halley nodded seriously.

Avalon couldn't help but smile. At least she and Halley could agree on *something*. It made Avalon feel like she'd been wearing someone else's clothes for the past two weeks and was now back in her favorite old sweats.

"Let's kick booty," Avalon added, putting on her best take-no-prisoners look.

"Yeah!" Halley snarled back with the same nose-wrinkle-slash-eye-squint.

The girls high-fived each other and took their positions. Constance served the ball straight to Avalon.

"Set!" Avalon called, lightly bouncing the ball up in the air so Halley could spike it perfectly. Across the net, Abigail got a face full of sand when she dived for the ball.

"Not funny." Abigail stood and brushed the sand off her pants. "But good shot, kiddo."

Inspired by the last play, Avalon proceeded to ace her first serve—and her second and third. Several rallies later, Team Halvalon was giddily in the lead, the girls shooting each other "Nice one!" and "Awesome spike!" kudos.

Avalon looked at her mom's and Abby's self-satisfied smiles through the little squares of the net and wondered if one volleyball game could really fix everything that had been broken. She and Halley were different people now, with different friends and different interests, and they'd done more awful things to each other in two weeks than friends ought to do in a lifetime. How could they really hope to undo all the damage now—if ever?

 **sms**
Daily

The official cyberzine of **Seaview Middle School**

SCHOOL NEWS   HEALTH   SPORTS   ENTERTAINMENT   **COMPETITION**

Dressed to Thrill
by Style Snark B

posted: saturday, 9/27, at 9:15 a.m.

All right, party people. Rumor has it there are some seriously happening soirees taking place tonight—one of which is hosted by yours truly and my fellow-snark, A. If you've been lucky enough to be invited to an A-list event (like ours!), here's the ultimate list of Dos and Don'ts for hitting those parties in style. I know what I'll be wearing . . . and you've still got time to try to keep up! So take note:

DO: Rock an ensemble nobody's ever seen before.
DON'T: Assume it'll look brand-new just because you've never worn it to school.

DO: Something funky with your hair (crimped, straightened, blowout, updo!).
DON'T: Interpret *funky* as skipping the shower and shampoo. Only a lucky few follically blessed can get away without daily shampoos, mmmkay?

DO: Make a bold statement (cool prints, bright colors, an off-the-shoulder top, sparkles, beads, or sequins).
DON'T: Over- or underdo it. (Ditch the accessories with a beaded dress, but bring on the bling with a simple strapless number.)

DO: Emphasize your personal style—fun and flirty or rock-star dirrrty?
DON'T: Test-drive a completely new look—style-schizophrenia makes us *all* feel crazy.

Above all, remember to work the room like it's the ultimate red carpet event—a movie premiere, an awards show, whatever. You never know when the paparazzi might be snapping a picture and running it on the front page of this very Webzine!

Word to your closet,
Halley Brandon

Can't wait for tonight! Glad 2 hear U and Avalon are back to BFF-ing (kind of! ☺).

posted by luv2gossip **on 9/27 at 9:32 a.m.**

Even this girl wants to look more princess than tuff tonight. Thanks for the good advice.

posted by tuffprincess **on 9/27 at 9:38 a.m.**

Party on, Snark B. See you and A 2nite.

posted by cheeriously **on 9/27 at 9:47 a.m.**

I love happy endings.

posted by realitease **on 9/27 at 10:11 a.m.**

Reunited (and it feels so good)

*H*alley stared at Avalon, her blond head framed by the limousine's interior neon lights. The solo limo ride was the first of several surprises The Moms had planned for the party, and the girls weren't quite sure what to say to each other.

This must be what it feels like to go on a first date, Halley thought while staring down at the mini-fridge sitting between her and Avalon. *Should I offer her a drink?*

As Halley breathed in the scent of new-car leather mixed with the clean, sweet smell of her and Avalon's favorite fragrance—Chanel Mademoiselle—she tried to focus on everything that had gone right in the past couple of days. They'd pummeled The Moms in the beach volleyball game, they'd smiled at each other in school a few times yesterday, they'd spent the evening helping The Moms get most of the party supplies assembled. . . . But now, they were wallowing in friendship limbo: There was no going back to the way things used to be, but they didn't quite know how to move forward, either.

"You look awesome," Avalon finally said, placing her hands carefully on her lap.

"Thanks." Halley smiled. She was wearing a pale blue chiffon babydoll dress. "You look like an Oscar."

"That's what I thought when I saw it!" Avalon beamed down at her Bebe gold sequined tank dress. "Do you think I should have worn my hair up, though?"

"Nooo." Halley shook her wavy brown locks. "I love that we both wore it down. Most people will probably be doing something funky like I suggested in my column."

"True."

Avalon and Halley exhaled at the same time and then laughed at their awkward synchronized breathing.

"Ohmygod, why am I so nervous?" Halley finally asked, raising a berry-painted fingernail to her mouth—primed and ready to bite.

"I am, too!" Avalon grinned, reaching across the limo's tan interior to pull Halley's hand away from her mouth. Halley smiled her thanks to Avalon for saving her new manicure.

"I've been trying not to have any expectations, but I just want tonight to be perfect," Avalon added, crossing her legs and flipping one of her gold platform sandals on and off her foot.

"Me, too," Halley agreed. She wasn't just nervous about being alone with Avalon. She was also battling the swarm of Wade-inspired butterflies in her stomach. She'd even had a dream about him last night, in which he'd gently guided her to a secluded corner of the rooftop patio and, with nothing but the moon to illuminate his chiseled features and messy black hair shaped into just a hint of a fauxhawk, he had leaned down and given her her first *real* kiss.

Halley had been wanting to tell Avalon about the dream but wasn't sure how she'd react, so she kept it to herself.

Avalon reached for the gold-and-black beaded clutch sitting next to her on the limo seat and pulled out a small red box with a purple ribbon. "I got this for us."

Halley took the red box in her trembling hands. "For us?" she asked, her forehead creasing.

"Just open it." Avalon smiled.

Halley untied the white bow and pulled the top off the box. Inside were two delicate gold necklaces, each with a round dog tag engraved with the words BEST FRENEMIES.

Halley burst out laughing. It was too perfect. And crazy.

"I saw it yesterday and thought of you, well, us." Avalon blinked her golden-brown eyes at Halley.

"It's fabulous." Halley nodded as she helped Avalon put on her necklace, then turned so Avalon could return the favor.

"So . . ." Halley locked eyes with Avalon, whose eyes looked watery. Halley's nose began to tingle like she'd inhaled too many Diet Coke bubbles. But she didn't even want to *think* about what crying would do to their professionally applied makeup. "Truce?"

Avalon didn't say anything for several seconds. "To best frenemies!" she finally answered.

And that called for a party!

Surprise, surprise

The entire upstairs deck of Nate's had been transformed into a fashion show set. Avalon spun around in the balmy ocean air to take it all in. On the far end was the big white stage with a banner that read FRIENDAPALOOZA. Each letter was spelled with a different piece of designer fabric, like the Louis Vuitton monogram and the Chanel and Coach logos. Two giant *Teen Vogue* covers with pictures of Halley and Avalon and cover lines like BORN TO BE STYLED and FRIENDSHIP IS ALWAYS IN FASHION! flanked the sides. A long white runway extended from the front of the stage and down the center of a black-and-white checkered dance floor. Several platforms featured life-size cardboard cutouts of the girls in their favorite outfits through their lives. Heat lamps were set up everywhere, giving the cool evening a toasty, tropical feel, and colorful paper lanterns were strung between potted palm trees. As if the incredible decorations weren't enough, the sun was just about to set above the La Jolla coastline, cloaking the panoramic view in majestic dark blue and purple with streaks of fiery orange.

"How cute were we?" Halley smiled as she and Avalon walked past a display of their five-year-old selves.

Avalon ran her gold manicured fingertips along the little pink-and-green Pucci dress her mom had had custom-made for her when she was three. "We were the best dressed babies on the planet."

"Pretty great, huh?" beamed Avalon's mom, who looked beyond chic in a strapless red-and-gold Nicole Miller sheath, her platinum bob swept back on one side with a diamond-encrusted clip.

"But check *this* out," Abigail said, clapping her hands. She was a vision of bohemian hip in a brightly colored silk spaghetti-strap scarf dress.

The Moms grabbed each other's hands and walked the girls over to the stage. They craned their heads up at the giant-screen TV playing a loop of home movies.

"Oh! Remember that birthday party?" Halley draped a bronzed arm around Avalon's sun-kissed shoulders.

"How could I forget?" Avalon laughed at the images of her and Halley getting tossed into the Greenes' pool after a chocolate cake fight. "We look so *little* there!"

"Okay, one last surprise." Constance smiled as she and Abigail led the girls over to the white leather DJ booth, where a guy in giant, black padded headphones was pulling out albums and adjusting something on his sleek, silver MacBook Pro.

"This is B-Minus," Abigail announced, ruffling her long fingers through her auburn hair and then whispering to the girls: "DJ AM had an emergency wedding to work, but he said B taught him everything he knows—"

"Hey, hey, hey!" the DJ said in a muddled accent that could have come from France, Spain, or Italy. He slid the headphones down around his neck, shifted his shoulders back, and pointed his index fingers at the girls.

Avalon looked over at Halley and silently begged her not to make her laugh. The guy had feathered dirty-blond hair, a nose to rival Owen Wilson's, a weird stripy orange tan, and the most bizarre pattern of facial hair. And his white silk shirt provided a little too much information about the obscene quantity of chest hair he possessed.

"Thank you *so* much," Avalon and Halley said in unison as they entered into a big group hug with The Moms. Then they quickly shooed the parents downstairs, where they'd promised to be for most of the night.

As people began arriving, no one mentioned the Halvalon breakup-and-reconciliation. Then again, there were so many other things to look at and talk about, and it was pretty obvious that the girls were back in sync. Avalon's face started to hurt from smiling so much.

"Great party!" Brianna said, hugging Halley and Avalon as one of the waitresses shimmied by with a silver tray full of crab cakes.

"Isn't it so fun?" Halley responded. Avalon was stoked that Halley was being nice to Brianna, even though the cheer captain was kind of a No on this particular night in a bright yellow, strapless floor-length princess dress. Prom, anyone?

"This is so awesome!" Sydney widened her violet eyes excitedly. She didn't look like a cheerhuahua tonight. She looked more like a porcelain doll with her hair straightened and an adorable teal empire-waist dress. "Love the music!"

"Thank you!" Avalon glanced over at the crowd dancing on either side of the catwalk.

Halley grinned, biting into a mini fish taco. She crumpled up a white cocktail napkin personalized with FRIENDAPALOOZA in glittery blue and brown and then started a little as she looked toward the entrance.

"What?" Avalon asked.

"Oh, it's just—" Halley began.

But Avalon saw exactly what Halley was looking at: The Dead Romeos had entered the building. "You should go say hi," Avalon told her. She was no great fan of Sofee, who looked barely passable in a T-shirt dress and platform espadrilles, but this night was about being a good friend.

"I should," Halley said. "Thanks," she added before squeezing Avalon's hand and heading toward her new friends.

Around nine o'clock, Avalon watched her best friend walk onstage, where the Dead Romeos had just finished setting up their equipment.

"Hey, everyone," Halley said into the microphone as she smiled out at the crowd. "Avalon and I want to thank you for coming. We hope you're all having a good time."

Avalon was so proud of her friend—she looked stunning and confident.

"Well, we've got a lot more in store," Halley continued, leaning into the microphone with a big smile. "Not only am I proud to introduce the Dead Romeos for a live set, but I'm psyched to premiere their very first video—directed by me, of course!"

As everybody cheered, Mason clapped his drumsticks together and yelled, "Ah one, ah two, ah one, two, three, four!"

The Dead Romeos broke into song, Wade crooning into the microphone. Even Sofee looked cool with her cherry-red guitar.

And then Avalon paid attention to the music video playing on the gigantic screen set up behind the band. Except it didn't look like something you'd see on MTV. It didn't even look like something you'd see on VH1.

Because it was of Avalon.

She looked up to see *herself* performing her floor routine at gymnastics practice—the day she left the team. In slow motion. The Dead Romeos continued playing in front of the screen, and Avalon's boobs bounced in time to the song's hook.

Avalon froze as her chest filled the plasma TV. It felt like she was suddenly in a circus funhouse, minus the fun. Everyone's voices sounded distorted and creepy, and their faces looked like they were stretching out and wiggling balefully at her. They all appeared to be laughing, and why wouldn't they be? She was a walking freak show, an eighth-grader with an alleged boob job!

It was one thing to make fun of Avalon's boobs in a column, but quite another to blow them up and slow them down on a TV screen at a party. *Her* party!

Halley had officially put the *enemy* in frenemy.

Avalon saw Brianna, Sydney, and most of the other cheerleaders giving her wide-eyed, *What are you gonna do?* looks. Even Lizbeth from journalism mouthed the words, "Are you okay?" as her pink crimped hair waved in the dark ocean breeze. Avalon took a deep breath, straightened up, and pasted a cheerleader-perfect smile on her face. No one, especially Halley, was going to see her cry.

"Nice rack," hollered a male voice as Avalon pushed her way onto the stage.

Avalon did some deep breathing. The whole thing was obviously just a part of Halley's twisted plan.

She might have thought she'd won, but then Halley had obviously forgotten everything about her former best friend—like the fact that Avalon would never, ever go down without a fight.

Crush and burn

Halley was trapped in a mass of bodies, unsure of which direction she should be heading. Part of her wanted to run straight across the rooftop deck, down the stairs, and out to the limo, while another part wanted to try to throw the DVD player into the Pacific. How had this happened? Where was her beyond amazing video? Clearly, she'd downloaded the wrong file to bring with her tonight, but of all the non-music video files to cue up, why did it have to be the one of Avalon at gymnastics practice?

Halley finally pushed to the stage, but just as she got to the edge of the catwalk, she saw a flash of gold and stopped short. She watched Avalon walk determinedly to the DVD player and press STOP.

The Dead Romeos stopped playing, confused looks on all their faces. Avalon grabbed the microphone from Wade.

"All right!" Avalon nodded her head enthusiastically and pumped her arms in the air like the football team had just scored a touchdown. "Was that *awesome* or what?"

Halley couldn't believe her ears.

"So, for those of you still wondering . . . Yes, they are real!" Avalon laughed a little too loudly, pushing out her chest so far that the stage lights reflected off her boobs and created a double-disco-ball effect.

"It's the Golden Globes!" a male voice called from somewhere in the middle of the crowd, which generated some more whistles and cheers, mostly from the guys.

Avalon giggled in a way Halley had never heard before.

"I'm so sorry to interrupt the Dead Shakespeares. I mean Romeos . . . but before they play the rest of their set, Halley and I have one more surprise for you all."

Halley was still frozen in place. Where was Avalon going with all this? Was she actually happy about the attention the video seemed to be getting her? Come to think of it, Avalon *had* been flaunting her chest in front of Wade. Was this the new *cheerleader* version of Avalon— the one Halley hadn't really hung out with for more than two weeks?

"Halley . . . come on up here!" Avalon searched the crowd until she finally locked eyes with Halley.

People were giving Halley little jabs in the back, whispering for her to go on. She tentatively stepped up onto the stage and stood next to Avalon, shrugging at the crowd to let them know that she was just rolling with the punches.

"We've been dying to sing for you guys all night, and well . . ." Avalon looked over at Halley with a huge smile. "Halley actually wrote her own song—about a certain special someone. So listen closely to the lyrics. We hope you love it as much as *she* loves *him*! DJ, could you cue up 'Beautiful'?"

As the sound of the familiar Christina Aguilera song began playing, Halley broke out in a cold, panicked sweat. B-Minus walked over and handed Halley a microphone, which she held limply at her side.

Halley felt like her feet were stuck in cement blocks and her throat was filling up with cotton balls—the extra-puffy cosmetic kind. A searing wave of queasiness rippled through Halley's stomach, up to her throat, and back down again. She knew the Dead Romeos were standing directly behind her, and she could practically feel Wade's eyes burning into her back as Avalon said, "Come on, Hal—if you don't sing it, I guess I'll just have to." Then Avalon crooned over Christina's voice:

"Oh, Wade, you're beautiful, so beautiful today.
I'm stoked you moved to town . . .
Yes, Wade, you're beautiful in every single way.
So glad we finally found . . .
. . . all of the love we found today."

Halley couldn't believe Avalon had actually remembered—and just *repeated*—the words Halley had been singing in *private*.

She didn't want to turn around and see the Dead Romeos laughing at her. She didn't want to make eye contact with the throngs of people cheering for Avalon or looking at Halley like she was a tragic, lovesick groupie. She just wanted to make the whole night disappear, and figured that fleeing the scene would be a start.

Halley dropped her mic and bolted down the runway as the speakers screeched a deafening shriek. When she reached the end of the catwalk, she just kept on running.

Cheers and jeers

Avalon gazed out a window at the moon shimmering on the dark ocean off in the distance. She was hiding out in the far corner of a smaller downstairs room at Nate's, stretched out on a pale wood bench, clutching one of the ivory pillows. The sounds of her parents' laughter and clinking dishes and the faint buzz of the Dead Romeos playing upstairs just made her feel more depressed. As Avalon twisted a lock of long platinum hair around her index finger, her mind raced.

Why had Halley played Avalon's gymnastics routine instead of the Dead Romeos' video—and why had she done it when things seemed to be going so much better between them? Would Avalon ever be able to show her face in school again—and if she did, would people even look her in the eye, or just at her grotesquely enormous boobs?

She had put on a good show, pretending that Halley's video stunt hadn't bothered her. But deep down, she felt like her world was coming apart at the seams. And not just over what Halley had done to her, but also over what she had done to Halley. She kept trying to tell herself that Halley had deserved what she got, that Halley had been asking for it. But somehow it wasn't helping.

"Hey, everyone's been asking for you." Brianna floated into the room like a bright-yellow fairy godmother and sat down on the bench near Avalon's bare feet. "I thought you'd just taken a bathroom break or something."

Avalon frowned and hugged the pillow tighter to her chest, causing the gold sequins on her dress to dig into her skin. "Why would anybody up there want to hang out with me now?"

Brianna tilted her head and fixed her dark almond eyes on Avalon's. "That *was* a pretty harsh performance."

"How could she *do* that to me?" Avalon asked, casting her eyes down to the gray-carpeted floor where she'd kicked off her gold platform sandals. "I mean, how devious can one person possibly *get*?"

Brianna looked at Avalon sideways. "I think everybody thought the video was kind of funny—like a joke between you and Halley or something. I mean, you did such a good job of laughing it off. And your gymnastics routine *was* incredible."

Avalon couldn't believe Brianna was trying to make this about her tumbling skills. "It looked like the winning clip from *America's Bustiest Home Videos*."

Brianna fluffed the yellow chiffon material on her skirt. "See? You can still joke about it, which just goes to show it wasn't all *that* bad. But Halley . . ." Brianna trailed off. "I mean, I don't know what I'd do if somebody majorly outed my crush while he was standing right there."

Avalon didn't know what to say. She wanted to point out that Halley had started it, but that made her feel like she was seven years old and trying to argue her way out of a punishment.

"I just"—Brianna shrugged her shimmer-dusted bare shoulders and shook her head pensively—"I thought you and Halley were friends."

"We *were*," Avalon said, practically digging a gold finger-nail into the back of the wood bench, "until she showed that video. What kind of person does that?"

"But two wrongs don't make a right," Brianna noted, widening her eyes earnestly. "You should have just taken the high road. That's what I thought you were going to do until you sang that song."

With anybody else, Avalon would have immediately snarked on how ridiculously cliché the conversation-slash-lecture had become. But this wasn't just anyone. And if her life was going to remain Halley-less, Avalon needed Brianna on her side more than ever.

Brianna leaned in again, preparing to impart more of her wisdom. "Think of positive versus negative energy. Cheerleading is about being positive. And when one squad member does something negative, it makes us all look bad. What you did to Halley goes against everything we stand for."

But what about all the cheers that contained the word *fight* or taunted the other team? Wasn't cheerleading about winners versus losers? Besides, what about Halley and *her* negative energy? Hadn't Avalon just defended herself against the beyond-offensive Halley Brandon?

"Just something to think about," Brianna concluded before standing up to leave.

Avalon wanted to call after her. Was she in some kind of actual trouble with the team? Why couldn't Brianna see things from Avalon's perspective? If Brianna didn't understand Avalon, and Halley didn't understand Avalon, who did—and who ever *would*?

And just like that, Brianna's yellow skirt disappeared up the stairs, along with Avalon's hopes to fill her now *very vacant* best friend slot.

The one that got a Wade

In through the nose, out through the mouth, in through the nose, out through the mouth. Halley closed her eyes and focused on breathing the way her mom's private yoga instructor had taught her. Every time she inhaled, she caught a whiff of the limousine's new-car smell.

It had been a half hour since Halley had bailed on the party. Every time she considered heading back inside, she could practically hear the laughter and ridicule she'd endure over Avalon "Aguilera" Greene's rendition of "Beautiful."

Halley ran her fingers along the buttery leather seat of the limo and reflected on how the evening *could* have gone:

She'd spot Wade across the party, his dark eyes twinkling at the sight of her. He'd tell her how great she looked, and then they'd joke about adding a couple of Wiggles songs to the Dead Romeos set. He'd ask her to look over a new song he'd just written, and then, reading the lyrics, she'd realize it was a love song. A love song about her. And just as they were about to kiss, Mason would yell, "Crab cakes! I love see-food!"

Halley forced the image of Mason out of her head and returned to the vision of Wade gazing down at her. And that's when they would finally kiss.

The sudden whoosh of the limo door opening startled Halley back into reality. She blinked a few times as Sofee climbed into the car, her minidress clinging to her legs gracefully as she slid onto the tan seat opposite Halley.

"You scared me," Halley said with a half smile.

"Oh, is *that* why you ran out of the party?" Sofee grinned.

"Uh, no." Halley was actually grateful for the joke. Perhaps there would be a way to laugh the whole thing off after all. Maybe Sofee was even there to deliver a message from Wade? Maybe he thought the whole thing was funny? Maybe he even liked the song? Maybe he really had written something for her, too? She looked at Sofee hopefully.

"We played our set," Sofee told her instead. "People really like it."

"I'm sorry I missed it." Halley frowned. She tilted her head so her long wavy brown hair fell in front of her face.

"Yeah, well . . ." Sofee sighed. "I can kind of understand why you left."

Halley stared down at Sofee's platform espadrilles, unsure of what to say next.

"If I were you, I would *kill* Avalon."

"Believe me, I'm considering it." Halley managed a smile.

"Well, the good news is that Wade thinks you're awesome."

Halley's heart raced. This was it! Sofee *was* there to deliver a message. Maybe Wade was standing right outside the limo, just waiting to be invited in. Halley might even have to *thank* Avalon.

"And I do, too," Sofee continued, pausing for what felt like an eternity. "And so do Evan . . . and Mason. But the thing is. Well . . ."

What? What? WHAT?

"God, I should have told you this sooner." Sofee suddenly sounded nervous.

"WHAT?" Halley finally demanded, unable to wait any longer.

"Um. Wade and I are kind of . . . seeing each other."

Halley fell back against the seat. Wade and Sofee were a *couple*?

"I know, I know." Sofee shook her head apologetically. "I mean, it only just happened in the past week or so. I wanted to wait to say something until I was sure it was real. You know, bad luck or something."

"Well, that makes sense," Halley said slowly. Sitting next to Sofee, she felt like a kid in her pale blue babydoll dress. "I mean, that's awesome. I'm really happy for you."

Sofee leaned toward Halley. "But, the song—?"

"Ohmygod," Halley giggled and threw her head back for effect. "I totally made that up as a joke." As soon as the words came out of her mouth, Halley realized it was the most implausible little white lie in the history of little white lies.

Sofee raised her eyebrows at Halley—one of which had a brand-new tiny silver hoop in it.

Maybe she *was* a pierceaholic.

"I swear!" Halley practically shouted, hoping that increased volume would make her words sound more convincing. "I totally don't have feelings for *your* boyfriend."

"Okay, cool." Sofee nodded and smiled, but Halley could tell she didn't really believe her. "I'm sorry if this makes things weird."

"Not at all." Halley shook her head vigorously. "In fact, I was planning on inviting you to sleep over tonight after the party, because I wanted to show you the *real* video I made for you guys. That other one was obviously an accident."

"Yeah, I was wondering what happened to that." Sofee laughed. "But . . . um . . . we have a million things to do tonight. Maybe another time?"

"Sure." Halley forced a smile as Sofee slid toward the limo door and carefully stepped out.

Sofee waved and closed the door, leaving Halley alone with her thoughts. There were only three:

That no amount of breathing exercises or fantasies were going to clean up the disaster that was her life.

That she needed a serious plan for getting revenge on Avalon *and* rehabilitating her own reputation.

And that she had no time to lose.

This Is Not a Love Song
by Style Snark B

posted: sunday, 9/28, at 9:01 a.m.

Apparently this has become the weekend for speaking our minds and confessing our innermost feelings, and perhaps some of you are now privy to the fact that I have a penchant for putting my own thoughts to the beat of popular tunes. For those of you who had a front-row seat to last night's karaoke hack job, you should know that the lyrics were an outdated joke. But this one's brand-new, totally true, and just for you, Style Snark A. If you're up for another performance, just pop in your old No Doubt album and rock on. . . .

Underneath It All
There's times when I want to tell you just where to go, oh.
There's times when this "friendship" of ours seems superfaux.
And you hide true colors in you like no one else.
And below that pep squad sweater, something really smells.

You're really ugly—underneath it all.
Vicious, not bubbly—underneath it all.
Your legs are stubbly—underneath it all
You're really ugly—underneath it all.

That's it for now, everyone. Hope you're having a great weekend. We'll give you a complete fashion wrap-up from the hottest parties in town mañana. Till then . . .

Word to your closet,
Halley Brandon

COMMENTS (232)

Dude, that wasn't even harsh enough for what happened at the partay. You go, Hal. And remember: There's nothing wrong with having a crush on the hottest guy in school. I'm backing you one-hundy-and-ten!

posted by rockgirrrl **on 9/28 at 9:12 a.m.**

I heard U got what U deserved after making a B movie. Or was it a double-D movie? D'oh! But I do have one more word 4 U: YOUTUBE!

posted by luv2gossip **on 9/28 at 9:39 a.m.**

How R we supposed to keep up with all this? R U back 2gether or not? And where's the fashion advice?

posted by superstyleme **on 9/28 at 9:46 a.m.**

The official cyberzine of **Seaview Middle School**

SCHOOL NEWS | HEALTH | SPORTS | ENTERTAINMENT | **COMPETITION**

Weekend Update
by Style Snark A

posted: sunday, 9/28, at 9:52 a.m.

Please disregard the previous post from my co–Style Snark.
She will be checking into a mental health facility this afternoon
and we ask that you respect her privacy during this difficult
time.

Shop on,
Avalon Greene

Ha! I guess I'd need professional help after that song U sang, too—or maybe I'd just transfer to a new school. From Friendapalooza . . . to FriendapaLOSERS!

posted by luvshaq **on 9/28 at 9:57 a.m.**

Is it true that you'll be auctioning off your bras to raise money for H's treatment? U should. It's the least U could do.

posted by justinsgirl **on 9/28 at 10:12 a.m.**

Never reveal a friend's crush . . . what u did was un4givable. Team Halley 4 Life!

posted by madameprez **on 9/28 at 10:29 a.m.**

4get Mark Cohen's column, this is clearly where the gloves really come off. I want more!

posted by tuffprincess **on 9/28 at 10:31 a.m.**

Blame it on the rain

A flash of lightning illuminated Avalon's room and woke her from her Sunday-afternoon nap. The rain sounded like somebody was hurling rocks against the arched picture window of her bedroom. She breathed in the sweet, citrusy smell of the triple-wicked Voluspa candle that sat burning on her vanity table. Its flames were casting long, sinister shadows on the framed fashion magazine covers hanging on her ivory walls.

All she wanted to do was stay snuggled up under her honey-and-cream-striped Italian comforter and sleep away the rest of the school year. But a firm knock on her bedroom door assured her that wasn't an option.

"What?" Avalon padded across the plush white carpet, mumbling to herself. She was stunned silent when she flung open the door.

227

"Downstairs," her mom said firmly. "Now."

"Why?" Avalon tried not to sound annoyed. Avalon hadn't even told her parents what happened last night, just that she wanted to ride home with them instead of in the limo with Halley.

"Just move it," Constance replied flatly, turning on the heels of her black leather mules and walking purposefully down the hall. "Everyone's waiting."

"Who's everyone?" Avalon asked as she followed her mom down the dark wood stairs.

Before they even got to the bottom step, Avalon had her answer. There, sitting on the oversize burgundy sofa were Halley and her parents, with Avalon's dad in one of the matching chairs. And no one was looking at Avalon. That's because in the chair next to Martin Greene sat none other than Miss Frey.

Avalon felt like someone had turned the thermostat up beneath her charcoal-gray Hard Tail hoodie. Sweat crept down her back.

"Um, hi, Miss Frey." Avalon's voice cracked. She quickly cleared her throat and ran her palms along her pants.

"Hi, Avalon." Miss Frey offered her a tight smile. She was dressed down—for her—in a pair of camel-colored gaucho pants and a long white tunic top with a wide black leather belt and gunmetal flats.

There was nothing weirder than seeing teachers outside

their natural academic habitat. It was like a stars-without-makeup magazine feature—it shattered the mystery.

There were five white mugs on the coffee table in the middle of the room, and three half-eaten plates of grapes and cookies sat on a silver tray. Apparently the adults had been chatting for a while. Avalon looked over at Halley, who was flanked by her parents and staring down at the rug. Her hair was wet and her faded jeans and long-sleeved black T-shirt were sticking to her slender frame. She must have walked over in the rain.

"Why don't you sit here?" Martin suggested to Avalon, standing up and motioning for her to take the chair he'd been sitting on.

Avalon picked a misshapen grape to stare at on the table, avoiding looking at Halley at all costs.

"So, I'm really sorry—again—to interrupt your morning like this," Miss Frey said when everyone was finally seated. Her voice cut through the silence in the room.

"Oh, please don't apologize," Constance replied immediately, shooting a quick glare in Avalon's direction. "We're sorry *your* Sunday's being spent like this."

Miss Frey shrugged and grimaced as she pushed herself onto the front edge of her chair. "Well . . . Halley, Avalon. I've already gone through all the details with your parents." Miss Frey looked tortured—like a reality show contestant who knows she's about to get sent home. "I was hoping I wouldn't have to do this the night before the big vote, but because you've blatantly ignored my warning . . ."

Avalon wrapped her right hand around her thick blond ponytail and began to tug. Miss Frey didn't need to continue. She knew what was about to happen.

"I'm going to have to disqualify you," Miss Frey almost whispered, as if it was difficult for her to utter the words out loud.

Avalon stole a quick glance at Halley, but she was still sitting there like a mannequin, staring at the ground. Avalon was afraid to look at her parents, so she turned her brown eyes toward Pucci, who was peacefully curled up and asleep in front of the fire. Oh, to be a puppy.

"I'm sorry," Miss Frey said. "But you've really left me no choice."

Avalon heard Halley's mom clear her throat as if she was going to say something, but the room remained uncomfortably silent except for the rain pelting down on the roof and the faint sound of Pucci snoring.

"We're sorry, too," Martin said. Avalon looked over at her father just in time to see him frown and shake his head.

Losing Halley hadn't only cost Avalon a best friend. Now it had killed her fashion column, her social life, her academic record. The list went on.

Sorry didn't even begin to cover it.

The way we were

Tears streamed down Halley's face as she sat in her modern white bed and ate Pop Secret kettle corn. She grabbed the silver remote for her flat-screen HDTV off the bedside table and turned up the volume so she could hear every word of the home movies The Moms had put together for the party.

It felt like ages since she'd laughed herself to tears.

On screen, The Moms were dressed in knee-high boots and Pucci minidresses and they were dancing around the Greenes' living room, holding their Santa-hat-clad infant daughters. They swung the girls around and struck a bunch of poses that were almost identical to the moves Halley and Avalon usually threw down when they had one of their worst-dancer-of-the-night sleepovers. But The Moms really danced that way and thought it looked *good*. Halley couldn't figure out how she and Avalon had done so well in gymnastics with such rhythmically challenged parents.

Halley's laughter was like an emotional massage, kneading away the stress knots in her neck and shoulders. At least losing the *Daily* column competition would mean Halley didn't have to read any more scathing Style Snark A posts or come up with new ways to fire back. Even after claiming her feelings for Wade weren't depicted accurately, she couldn't stop herself from thinking about him.

As she reflected on Wade's visit to her house, to this very room—tracing a heart on the window right over there—Halley couldn't help but wonder if Wade and Sofee were really all that serious. Halley raised her arms and began rubbing her palms along the back of her neck and shoulders, willing the images of Sofee and Wade together to disappear from her mind. But they weren't going anywhere.

In front of her, the TV screen jumped to a sixth-grade graduation barbecue in the Greenes' backyard. As the eleven-year-old versions of Halley and Avalon laughed, Halley thought about the friendship they were supposed to have been celebrating last night, and how horribly wrong it had all gone.

Her eyes began to burn with tears again, but this time there was nothing funny about them. She jumped off the bed, walked over to the sliding-glass doors leading out to her patio, and flung them open. Everything was dark. And then she saw a light flick on and off from Avalon's room. Was Avalon sending her their pre–cell phone signal? Did she want Halley to come over? Did she want to make up?

Halley stared at the Greenes' house, but the windows remained dark—including Avalon's. Halley was the only Brandon home. Their parents had decided to take Tyler and Courtney out to dinner, leaving the girls all alone as phase one of their punishment.

Halley took one last look at Avalon's window and realized she had probably just gone to sleep. But in the distance, she thought she heard whistling, and then stomping down the hallway. Halley held her breath and stepped back inside.

With a gust of wind, her bedroom door flew open.

A lost cause

"Ohmygod, didn't you hear me calling your name?" Avalon yelled at Halley, who was standing near her balcony, looking completely terrified. "Didn't you see the old signal?"

"I *knew* it!" Halley smiled. "But why didn't you just call me?"

"I *did*!" Avalon practically screamed, unable to contain her frustration. "Like a million times."

Halley jumped off her bed and walked over to her egg-shaped chair, fumbling around in her messenger bag until she found her cell phone. She hit a few buttons, then threw it back in her bag and shrugged.

"I guess I forgot to charge it."

Of course.

Avalon glared at Halley. Her oversize white Harry Potter

T-shirt and blue-and-yellow plaid flannel PJ bottoms were spotted with grease. If it weren't for her freshly washed long hair, Halley could have passed for her dorky older brother. Easily. It was too tragic for words.

"Okay, I'm *sorry!*" Halley widened her pale blue eyes, grabbed the remote off her popcorn-covered bed, and shut off whatever lame DVD she'd been watching. "Did you come over here just to harass me for my dead cell battery, or is there another reason for this unwelcome visit?"

"I so don't have time for this right now!" Avalon scanned the mountains of laundry on Halley's floor, the piles of books next to her desk, and the crumpled bag of microwave popcorn sitting on her bed. "*Where* is Pucci?"

"I don't know. You have custody tonight."

"Yeah, I'm aware of that," Avalon spat, tempted to throw open the pale wood doors of Halley's walk-in closet to see if she'd hidden the puppy in there. "But I've been searching my house for the past hour, and I can't find her anywhere. I assumed you abducted her as payback for getting disqualified . . . not that any of this has been my fault."

"You seriously think *I'm* the one to blame?"

Avalon couldn't even think about academic issues right now. She'd deal with those problems later. Her mind was completely consumed with Pucci's well-being—or lack thereof.

And just like that, Avalon wasn't angry—she was *terrified*.

Where else could Pucci be? Was she lost? Hurt? Avalon tried to stop the worst-case scenarios from flashing before her eyes, but she couldn't block out the image of Pucci's mangled body lying in the middle of a flooded road. She nearly burst into tears.

"I don't know who's to blame for anything right now," Avalon finally admitted, desperation nearly choking her. "All I know is that Pucci's missing. If she's not here, then I don't know where she is."

The girls ran through every room in the Brandons' house, flipping on lights, searching under beds, in bathrooms and closets. "Pucci! Pucci! Here, puppy! Come to Mommy!" The more they searched, the more frantic Avalon became. It became all too clear to her that Pucci wasn't at Halley's house. Pucci was lost. And they needed to come up with a game plan—fast.

Avalon's first instinct was to head home, create a quick flyer on her computer complete with all the cutest shots of the puppy, print up a hundred copies, and start going door-to-door. But she knew there wasn't time for all that. She looked Halley directly in the eyes when she spoke.

"Get your bike. Meet me out front. *Immediately!*"

The air was crisp and smelled like a beach campfire. Every house in La Jolla must have seized the opportunity to use their fireplaces for the first time in months. The girls rode up and down the cul-de-sacs of their hilltop neighborhood with the yellow glow of the streetlamps and a nearly full moon lighting their way.

An hour later, they were back at the curb in front of Avalon's house with no Pucci. Even in the dark, their tear-stains were visible. Avalon wiped her nose on the sleeve of her gray hoodie. It was time to go to Plan B.

"Let's make flyers and start knocking on the neighbors' doors," Avalon said, trying to keep calm. Panicking would accomplish nothing. "Or maybe we should skip the flyers and just go door-to-door."

"But it's after ten—on a Sunday."

"Well, what else can we do?" Avalon sobbed, still unable to shake the image of Pucci's limp, lifeless body from her mind. "We *have* to find her."

"Let's check your place one more time," Halley suggested. "Maybe The Moms are home from dinner and they'll know what to do."

Avalon agreed, mentally retracing her steps and wondering if she'd really checked every room in her house. But when the girls leaned their bikes in front of the Greenes' house and ran through the front door, they were met with silence and darkness. Nobody was home yet, and their screams for Pucci went unanswered. They dashed through the Greenes' kitchen and out onto the back patio. Avalon flipped on the pool lights. The clear blue water sparkled with no signs of a puppy at the bottom.

Avalon raced across the grass and through the gate dividing her backyard from Halley's. They both ran into the Brandons' yard, just as the rain started up again. Halley slammed the gate closed as they continued to scream for Pucci.

"It's no use," Avalon finally said, collapsing on the wet grass.

"We'll . . . find . . . her . . ," Halley insisted, each word coming out in a wet sob.

Both girls knelt on the muddy grass. Moisture seeped through Avalon's sweatpants, but she didn't care. Pucci was gone, her friendship with Halley was destroyed, and with the rain pelting down on them, it felt like nothing would ever be the same again.

"Wait!" Halley said, grabbing Avalon's arm. "Did you hear that?"

"Hear what?"

"That scratching . . . over there." Halley jumped up and pointed toward the old stone playhouse at the far end of the Brandons' yard.

"Are you *trying* to freak me out?"

"No," Halley insisted. "Come on."

Avalon shuddered. She felt like she was on the set of a horror film and was too scared to be left alone, so she followed Halley. Even if finding Pucci meant risking her own life, she was prepared to do whatever it took.

And they called it puppy love

Halley flung open the small wooden door of the playhouse and pulled Avalon in behind her. It was freezing, but at least it was dry. As Halley breathed in the musty old smell of her childhood, she detected the scent of something else—wet Pucci. They'd barely made it through the door when the puppy leapt up, practically knocking Halley to the ground and covering her face with sloppy wet kisses.

"Ohmygod! Pucci!" Halley began sobbing harder than she had all night. She couldn't remember ever feeling this kind of relief.

"It's really you!" Avalon was sobbing, too.

Halley reached out and pulled the three of them into a group hug. The girls were bawling and covered in dirt and sweat and tears, and it felt amazing. Nothing mattered anymore except that Pucci was okay.

"How did you get *in* here?" Avalon asked the dog through her tears. Halley braced herself for some sort of accusation, but it didn't come.

"Maybe she went outside to go potty and the thunderstorm scared her and she got confused about where she was," Halley offered. "If the playhouse door came unlatched, she could have thought it was our house and run in, and the wind could have closed the door behind her."

"Ohmygod." Avalon sounded terrified and clung more tightly to Halley's arm. "Doors opening and closing by themselves? Getting locked in here? Can we please go now?"

Halley couldn't help but laugh. This was where they sketched their very first fashion designs . . . where they sewed clothes for their Bratz dolls on a little pink plastic sewing machine . . . and where they promised each other they'd run their own fashion magazine. Halley slid her arm out of Avalon's grasp and reached down to squeeze her hand.

"We can go inside," Halley agreed, running her other hand along Pucci's wet and dirty fur. "But just tell me something first."

"Okay." Avalon sounded scared and hesitant.

"Do you remember all the designs we sketched here?"

"Of course," Avalon answered.

"And the original vintage *Vogue* vow? That we'd run our own fashion magazine? Do you remember all the promises we made each other?" Halley had to concentrate to keep her voice from cracking.

"Yeah." Avalon sounded small, sad. Almost apologetic. And it gave Halley hope.

"What happened to all that?" Halley asked. "To us?"

"I don't know."

"Are you sorry?" The words were out of Halley's mouth before she could stop them. She needed to know.

She could hear Avalon breathing in and out. But as the silence stretched between them, Halley began to wonder if she'd get an answer. Maybe Avalon didn't care anymore.

All of a sudden, Avalon's face crumpled, tears poured down her face. Finally, between sobs, Avalon gave in.

"I'm *so* sorry," Avalon admitted. "For everything. I'm so, so, so, so sorry."

Halley couldn't believe it. The Avalon she'd known since before she could walk, before she could dress herself, before she even knew what "best friends" meant, *never* apologized.

"Are *you* sorry?" Avalon asked quietly, her voice steadier.

Halley sighed and her eyes began tingling with fresh tears. She couldn't begin to find the words.

United we fall

To Avalon, the world smelled clean and delicious after a thunderstorm—like crisp, freshly laundered sheets. The sun was sparkling overhead; the cloudless sky looked even bluer than usual, and the grassy hills of SMS were so green the campus could have passed for a tropical Emerald City.

But this Monday morning would have been perfect no matter what. Avalon and Halley were back together. Pucci was safe and sound. They were one big happy family again, ready to handle whatever came their way.

After facing the possibility of never seeing Pucci again, Avalon had reevaluated what was really important to her. She had woken up knowing that it didn't matter that she and Halley were no longer the Style Snarks, that they'd lost the *Daily* competition, that her boobs were the laughing-stock of SMS, or even that she might get booted from the varsity cheerleading squad later today. All that mattered was that she had her best friend back.

As Halley and Avalon clutched each other's hands and walked along the brick footpath to first period, Avalon was convinced that anything was possible. She could sense it in the air.

"Great necklace," Avalon smiled over at Halley, whose wavy brown hair looked even shinier than usual. Her BEST FRENEMIES charm glinted from between the slit in her purple BCBG mandarin-collared top. Halley's entire outfit complemented Avalon's 7 For All Mankind denim shorts, pink ruffle-front shirt, and Juicy heart-charm flats perfectly.

"You too." Halley smiled back.

Avalon was determined not to let the last few weeks of bickering and betrayal go to waste. She and Halley would meet challenges head-on and rise above whatever stood in their way. She was pretty sure that when Brianna heard her new philosophy, she would realize that she needed Avalon just as much as Halley did.

"Hey!" Halley suddenly squeezed Avalon's hand. "What's going on up *there*?"

Avalon looked at the row of villas at the end of the brick footpath, with the ocean and cliffs off in the distance. As they approached their journalism class, they could see that the students who usually just milled around on the grass had divided into two separate groups. Avalon noticed some of them were holding signs and wearing matching shirts. Were they picketing or something? Maybe word had already gotten out about their *Daily* disqualification. Maybe their public wanted them back!

"Ohmygod—no way," Halley whispered when they were a few yards away.

There, on the left side of the footpath, the varsity cheerleaders and a dozen other people were wearing matching pink-sleeved raglan shirts. They all held signs that said things like "TEAM AVALON," "AVALON OR BUST," and "TEAM AVALON: WE SUPPORT OUR GIRL."

Brianna was right there in front, leading a chant: "Yes, she's got a super chest and Avalon is the best!" The pink-clad mass was shouting along behind her in perfect synch, trying to drown out the group opposite them.

Halley's side wasn't quite so organized, nor did they look as cute in their dark T-shirts. There were probably only about fifteen people, and their signs were smaller, some just scrawled on notebook paper—saying "TRUE LOVE WADES," "HALLEY'S GOT HEART," and "KEEP ON CRUSHING, HALLEY!" A little goth girl wearing a black jumper, black tights, and patent red Docs was leading a chant that was almost as pathetic as the signs: "Halley's cool! Let love rule!"

Avalon's eyes started to burn with tears as she realized all those pink-clad people were actually coming to her defense. Her defense for something *Halley* had done to her.

She shook her head, trying to erase all the Halley-the-horrible moments cycling through her mind: Halley mocking Avalon for being a cheerleader. Halley accusing Avalon of being fake . . . and having fake hair . . . and a fake tan . . . and fake boobs. Then there was Halley, sitting at her computer, writing a song about Avalon being vicious and ugly. And had Halley *really* been surprised to find Pucci in her creepy old shed last night, or had she been setting Avalon up, just like she'd set her up at the party on Saturday night?

"Avalon or bust," Halley snickered. "That's genius! Maybe we *should* put the video on *Boob*Tube."

BoobTube? Like a bad YouTube pun? Avalon dropped Halley's hand and turned to face her.

Could they really get past everything that had happened? Was Halley genuinely sorry for *all* of it? Halley's clear blue eyes had always vaguely reminded Avalon of the sky. But as she searched her best frenemy's face, Avalon realized that those eyes were exactly the color of the sky—right before a storm.

Acknowledgments

I owe a million thanks to Farrin Jacobs—not just for setting the ball in motion, but for the expertise that's kept it rolling—and to Josh Bank, for his wit and wisdom, and for taking a chance on (and believing in) me. I could not have done any of this without virtually every last editor I've met and worked with through the years—but three of the best made this particular project all possible, so *merci beaucoup* times infinity to Lanie Davis, Nora Pelizzari, and Sara Shandler.

I send huge, grateful kisses to the incredible community of writers out there—the ones I've admired from afar, the ones with whom I've worked directly, and the ones I'm fortunate enough to count as friends (Carolyn Mackler, Taylor Morris, and Rebecca Woolf, to name a few). I'm also indebted to Stacey Glick for all her early support, and to Jodi Reamer for being such a proactive, indefatigable, and patient pillar of strength.

A colossal thanks to my amazing family—particularly my parents, who become better friends to me every day (and have put up with more from me than they probably should!); my brother, who is a true inspiration; my little guy, Jack, who sweetens every day of my life; and Joel, who turned my world into a cheesy love song that I never want to stop singing. P.S. I love you, Sydney—even when you're being a yappy little cheerhuahua (which isn't all that often, really).

Finally, to all the fabulous females in my life, past and present: Thank you for making the good times even better and for smoothing out the rough patches.

Is Halvalon breaking up or making up?
Find out in

FAKETASTIC

a **FRENEMIES** *novel by alexa young*

Coming in July 2009

*Read on for a
sneak peek*

The Style Snarks

DON'T GET DRESSED WITHOUT US!

Party Fouls!

posted by avalon: tuesday, september 30, at 7:07 a.m.

If you were at the social event of the season on Saturday (thrown by yours truly), you probably already witnessed some of the public displays of *affliction* exhibited by a few of the questionably clad guests. But just in case you missed them (like that's possible), here's a quick rundown of the biggest NOs of the night:

1. **Heather "Pleather" Russell.** Sorry, Heddy, but you've been found guilty of raiding the Pussycat Dolls' closet. That shiny, tiny hiney-band belonged on your head, not your hips.

2. **Jenny "Fur-Ball" Morgan.** Please tell us that fuzzy collar was faux and you didn't actually do something desperate to the cute little chinchilla you brought in for show-and-tell at Muir Elementary. Either way, at least you'd have an alibi for the red marks you've been sporting on your neck ever since. We'd buy it. (The excuse, not the fur!)

3. **Tyla "Tutu Tutu Much" Walker.** Nice effort, sweetness, but we were hosting a fashion-themed fete, not auditions for *Swan Lake*.

Better luck next time, girls.

Word to your closet,
Halley Brandon

Shop on,
Avalon Greene

PS: Yes, the rumors are true: No matter what went down between us at the party, Halvalon is back and better than ever. YAY! ☺

PPS: Big props to you for finding the new home of Seaview Middle School's most worshipped column ever—where disqualification from the *Daily* competition for being überfierce obviously just made us hotter (and fiercer)!

COMMENTS (59)

Yippee! I knew you wouldn't stay broken up 4ever. This blog RULES! (And great party, btw. Did U like my dress??? Please say YES!)
posted by realitease on 9/30 at 7:23 a.m.

OMG. Seriously? I would never forgive someone who outed my crush. Halley, U R way 2 nice. I'll B waiting 4 U 2 kick Avalon back 2 the curb. Go, Team Halley!
posted by tuffprincess on 9/30 at 7:26 a.m.

Got 2 agree with tuffprincess. I'm not sure I believe you 2 made up, anyway. I mean, what Avalon did was totally un4givable.

posted by madameprez **on 9/30 at 7:29 a.m.**

Fierce-o-rama! The only thing hotter than this column was that crazy video of Avalon's gymnastics performance. Cannot believe how her boobs were jiggling to the Dead Romeos song. HILARIOUS! Glad to see U can laugh it off, Av. That's so, um, BIG of you. xoxoxo

posted by superstyleme **on 9/30 at 7:34 a.m.**

Well, I liked Tyla's tutu! But good call on the pleather and the fur-ball. (And FYI, Jenny's neck was courtesy of Jordan Campbell. The dude is a total vampiromaniac neck-mauler. Seriously. BTDT! :-O)

posted by luv2gossip **on 9/30 at 7:46 a.m.**

This blog sucks. For real reporting, check out the actual WINNERS of the *Daily* competition: Margie and Olive. Click <u>here</u> for their stupendous Disease of the Day column!

posted by dissect_this **on 9/30 at 7:59 a.m.**

BFFs are the new black

"Isn't it amazing?" Avalon Greene breezed up behind Halley Brandon and gave her best friend's shoulders an affectionate squeeze.

The girls' golden retriever mix, Pucci—named after their moms' favorite designer—followed Avalon into the room and leapt onto Halley's boho-fabulous bedspread, where she began slobbering all over her new Chewy Vuiton squeak-purse.

"Amazing times infinity!" Halley's clear blue eyes sparkled as she swiveled her white egg-shaped desk chair away from their brand-new Style Snarks home page and grinned up at Avalon. Their first post since breaking free from Seaview Middle School's cyberzine, the *SMS.com Daily*, shimmered gold and pink from the screen of Halley's iMac.

"Take *that*, Miss Frey!" Avalon scoffed, grabbing Halley's hands and pulling her up from her chair.

"And *that*, *Daily*-dot-lame competition!" Halley giggled.

The girls bounced up and down as Madonna's "Material Girl" began playing through the computer speakers. Halley picked up the remote and cranked the volume as she and Avalon launched into a dance routine that predated Avalon's recent move from the gymnastics team to the cheerleading squad. Pucci barked and chased them around the room until a sound barrier–defying screech stopped the girls in mid-kick–ball change.

"OH. MY. *GOD!*" Halley's older brother, Tyler, squealed. The pale high school sophomore stood in Halley's doorway, clutching the sides of his face with his hands.

"Hey, Tyler," Halley said patiently. She tilted her head and smirked, totally unfazed by his glass-shattering volume. "What's up?"

"I thought we were having an earthquake!" Tyler bulged out his eyes and shook his head in mock horror so that his wavy dark hair flopped around his lightly freckled face. "But it was just Halvalon: The Reunion Tour." Tyler put his hand on his hip and contorted his face into an exaggerated perky smile.

"Uh, you think *that* was scary?" Avalon replied tersely, about to comment on Tyler's golfer-gone-wrong ensemble. But then she remembered how helpful Tyler had been with setting up the Style Snarks site the previous night and made an abrupt detour.

"What's really scary is how *hot* you look today. I almost didn't recognize you. That shirt is, like, full-on *adorkable!*" Avalon grinned. It wasn't a complete lie. The sky blue polo matched Tyler's eyes almost exactly and, combined with the faded green cargo shorts and white Chuck Taylor low-tops, did achieve a sort of geek-chic je ne sais quoi.

"This old thing?" Tyler locked eyes with Avalon, strutted toward Halley's bed, and then pivoted, supermodel style. "I was thinking of you when I threw it on, Avvy," he added in a breathy voice. *"Ciao!"* And with a flamboyant wave, he was gone.

"Dude." Halley giggled and shook her head. "Could my brother be more of a spaz?"

"Seriously." Avalon grimaced as she pushed a sheath of long, pale hair behind her shoulder. "You are so lucky it's not genetic."

"Yeah, except he's pretty awesome when he uses his supergeek powers for the greater good," Halley noted as she walked over to her desk and sat down at her computer. "I mean, dork or not, Ty definitely delivered last night."

"True." Avalon followed Halley to the desk so she could take a closer look at their shiny new blog for at least the hundredth time since they'd created it.

It really was beyond gorgeous. The idea for the website had come to Avalon in a moment of extreme inspiration right before bed. She'd immediately thrown on her pink Barefoot Dreams robe and cozy Ugg slippers, raced through the gate separating her family's backyard from Halley's, and gone straight up to her best friend's room. Minutes after gleefully telling Halley her concept, Avalon had registered the domain name and gotten down to business, with Tyler helping out on the technical end. But as much as Avalon and Tyler had contributed, it was the picture Halley had sketched of both girls looking adorably horrified as they tossed ugly outfits into Pucci's eager, drooling mouth that made the site spectacular. It was perfect. No, it was better than perfect. It was snarktacular.

"I am *so* in love with the logo!" Avalon clasped her hands to her heart excitedly. She was convinced Style Snarks would be the talk of Seaview Middle School, if not the entire town of La Jolla and city of San Diego. Maybe they'd even become international sensations, known for their ferocious-but-fair fashion assessments! "Thank *God* you took that graphic design course at art camp."

"I knew it would come in handy." Halley smiled at her best friend.

"You were right—for a change." Avalon giggled. "Seriously, this blog is already *so* much better than our competition column, isn't it?"

"Absolutely." Halley nodded reassuringly and twisted a lock of her long, wavy dark hair around an index finger. "This might just be your best idea *ever*."

7

Avalon wrinkled her nose and shivered with anticipation. It had been weeks since she'd felt this happy. But now it seemed all the awful things that had happened since Halley got back from art camp had just made Halvalon stronger than ever. The moment Avalon had seen Halley's mod-a-licious ensemble this morning—a white peasant top under a black velvet vest with skintight Seven jeans and haute-pink-patent wedges—she'd been convinced her best friend was really back this time. All the weirdness that had threatened to destroy eighth grade was so completely last weekend.

"Ooooh, comments!" Halley announced after she turned back to the iMac and refreshed the page.

A giddy smile played across Avalon's face as she leaned over Halley's shoulder to read the responses to their debut post. She was expecting the enthusiasm of the first commenter to sweep across their readership. But with each word she read, she could feel more color draining from her face. The early feedback could not have been more anti-Avalon! A lump rose in her throat and she tried to cough it back down, just as Halley gasped audibly. They both laughed awkwardly to hide their simultaneous shock.

"Wow!" Avalon feigned delight while tugging at a lock of golden hair. "Looks like Team Halley found the site."

"What do you mean?" Halley turned and looked up, all wide-eyed innocence.

"What do you *think* I mean?" Avalon tried not to snap

at her best friend, but it was too late. She mashed her glossy lips together and then jumped onto Halley's bed to cuddle with Pucci. "You should *kick me to the curb* for outing your crush? The *hilarious* video of my gymnastics routine?"

"Dude." Halley rolled her eyes. "You had, like, fifty Avalon Teamsters cheering you on at school yesterday . . . *and* buying you lunch . . . *and* bringing you three different kinds of smoothies after cheer practice."

Avalon had to smile at that. Her supporters—led by pep squad captain Brianna Cho—had seriously rallied behind her. And Avalon couldn't help but feel sorry for her best friend when Team Halley's tragic attempt at support was blasting cheesy love songs in the middle of the quad. Halley must have been more embarrassed by hearing Christina Aguilera's "Beautiful" at lunch than she'd been by Avalon's impromptu performance of the song—slightly modified with Halley's crush-revealing lyrics—on Saturday night.

But now Avalon was worried. What if all their readers rallied around Halley? What if people thought Avalon was the villain, no matter how back on track she and Halley were? What if Team Avalon never found Style Snarks, or worse: What if they'd *disbanded*?

"Come on! Don't let it bum you out." Halley frowned emphatically. "This is exactly why creating our new blog is so important."

"Remind me of *exactly* why, again?" Avalon pouted as she rubbed Pucci's belly.

"Because now the whole school will see how recommitted we are to each other," Halley insisted, "and that we've united to save the school—one fashion disaster at a time!"

Avalon ran her fingers along Pucci's swirly orange and brown scarf, which complemented her own silky beige and tangerine-hued tank perfectly, and tilted her head in deep thought.

"Seriously!" Halley walked over to the bed to join Avalon and Pucci in a group hug. "Thanks to Style Snarks, *everyone* is going to be back on the same team: Team Halvalon for life! And it's all thanks to *you* for suggesting we start a blog."

Avalon finally returned her best friend's smile. Of course Halley was right. They'd always been unstoppable when they worked together. And now that they were reunited, nothing could get in the way of making eighth grade the best year of their lives.

Faketastic

from basic
to worstie
and back again

Alexa Young

Coming soon!